HEALING MISS MILLWORTH
THE SEDGEWICK LADIES
BOOK II

ISABELLA THORNE

Mikita Associates

PART I

CHAPTER 1

Miss Ellen Millworth paused for a single moment in the dim foyer of her home, as she returned from Lady Arabella Sedgewick's home. She took the extra time to fix a careful smile on her face. Her parents, she knew, would immediately and unconsciously search her expression the moment they set eyes upon her, and she would not for the world, cause them distress by showing anything but a pleasant smile. She could not recall a time in her life before where she had needed to school her expression into a smile. Indeed, according to family lore, she had been smiling almost since the moment of her birth.

But these last few months had brought a great many new and unpleasant experiences to her door, and having to order herself to smile was hardly the worst of her trials, she supposed.

"Oh, there you are darling, back from your visit with Arabella already?" Her mother, Mrs. Millworth, exclaimed, rising hastily the moment that Ellen stepped into the cozy parlor. "I had thought that you meant to spend the entire afternoon with the Sedgewicks." She poked her needle into her embroidery and put it aside to talk to her daughter.

How many times she did that, Ellen thought idly, put things aside for her. Moreso, lately, she realized. Ellen pulled off her gloves and sat down with her mother.

The room smelled like rosewood and the honeysuckle candles that were burning on the mantelpiece. The fire added an earthy, smoky smell.

"Arabella and I had a lovely visit, Mama," she said, "but we had to cut it short because the earl was called away unexpectedly and needed Arabella to entertain some visitors of his," Ellen explained, taking a seat near her mother. "Marianne offered to keep them occupied, but you know, Arabella is far too generous to allow her to suffer all afternoon, knowing how Marianne despises small talk." Ellen gave a small shiver and her mother noticed right away.

"I'll ring for some tea," she said. "You are no doubt chilled to the bone. It won't do for you to come down with an ague after all your trials."

Ellen did not want to speak of her trials. She nodded, anxious to hold a teacup, which would give her something to do with her hands.

Tea had become a daily ritual with her mother since Ellen was able to sit without randomly bursting into tears when thinking about her ordeal. She tried to put the matter and the man from her mind, but she could not suppress the shiver that accompanied the thought.

"It is cold outside," Ellen agreed. Tea would certainly warm her, but it was not cold that made her shiver. She didn't want to talk about her encounter with Sir James Randall, as her mother was wont to call it. The euphemism did not sit well with her. It wasn't an encounter or an incident. It was a kidnapping, although she had been somewhat complicit, she supposed. How could she ever have imagined herself in love with the villain? She felt soiled, just thinking of him. She shoved the thought away, changing the subject before her mother could go on about her victimhood. She couldn't bear it. She would concentrate on her friend and her friend's wedding, which was approaching with some speed.

"Marianne may as well start becoming accustomed to entertaining Lord Sedgewick's visitors now. The task will fall to her as soon as Arabella and Lord Willingham are married," Ellen said, keeping the conversation firmly on her best friend's events and not her own.

"Yes. I suppose that is true," Mrs. Millworth observed, in the indulgent tone in which she always spoke of the Sedgewick sisters. "Although, I daresay Arabella thinks to spare her as long as she can. I know she has resolved to stop shielding everyone from unpleasantness, but it's quite the long-standing habit with her, isn't it, to coddle her younger sisters?"

Ellen smiled. It was interesting her mother recognized the tendency in another and yet saw none of the coddling she herself did.

"I rather think it is more than a habit, for it seems to me to be a part of her very character," Ellen agreed, smiling genuinely at her mother now, and at the thought of her cousin and dearest friend, who had a tendency to shoulder the weight of the world as a matter of course. "Fortunately, I believe that Lord Willingham will help her find a sort of balance in that sort of thing. He adores her so. It is difficult for him to stand by idly and watch her put herself last."

"I must say, I am happy that your cousin Arabella found such a dear boy," Mother said as she poured the tea.

"Hardly a boy, Mama." Ellen stirred some cream and an inordinate amount of sugar into her cup.

"He *is* a dear boy, if I may be allowed to refer to a grown, to say nothing of titled, gentleman in such a manner. I am constantly delighted those two have found one another, aren't you?"

"I am," Ellen agreed, taking a sip of the hot tea which warmed her. She kept her fingers wrapped around the cup.

"How are preparations coming along for…" Mrs. Millworth suddenly trailed off, looking stricken. Ellen knew it was due to the fact that she had been about to mention the upcoming wedding between Lady Arabella Sedgewick and Lord Christopher Willingham.

"Mama, really, I hope I am not so delicate that I cannot bear to hear the word 'wedding'," Ellen said with a small amount of asperity. "You know how happy I am for Arabella, and so does she."

"Of course, my darling, of course I know that. I only hate to say anything that might cause you any distress. You know that Doctor Larkin cautioned your father and I against reminding you of…of recent events, at least until your unpleasant dreams cease to have such strength and frequency."

Ellen stared into her teacup, willing away the thoughts of her bad dreams, reflecting that she should not inflict the worry of those dreams upon her mother. She winced at the need to lie to Mama. She had never done so before in her entire life and did not want to do so now, but felt she must.

She laid this new outcome squarely on the lap of that blackguard. She would not name him. She would not even think of him. She cut him from her life and her thoughts. "I slept quite well last night, Mama," lied Ellen stubbornly. "Like a baby, in fact."

"You never cried in your sleep as a baby, as you have done recently," Mrs. Millworth pointed out quietly, looking at her daughter over her teacup. She knew Ellen too well and her steady gaze was piercing, despite its gentleness.

"I do not want you to have to be so constantly concerned over my state of mind, Mama," Ellen said, standing up from the tea table and moving closer to her mother. She wrapped her arms around the woman's thin shoulders. Mrs. Millworth had never been inclined to frailty, and Ellen realized that worry over her daughter's troubles had been affecting the woman even more than she had realized.

"Of all the foolish things to say," Mrs. Millworth exclaimed fondly, exhaling a shaky laugh. "Whatever else in the world would I concern myself with, my darling? Your happiness and well-being mean everything to your father and I, which is hardly a new development. You have always been the center of our lives."

Ellen winced. "I am blessed to have the most wonderful, doting parents in existence, I do believe," Ellen said, kissing her mother's cheek fondly. "You need not worry about me," Ellen asserted. "Truly."

"That is just what Doctor Larkin was saying to me only this morning. He called, you know, to bring by a sleeping tincture for you. We are terribly fortunate to have such a doctor nearby. I can't think of any other physician who had such a perfect combination of knowledge and compassion. His father would have gladly secured an officer's commission or an excellent living with a prosperous vicarage, you know, his family is quite established and well-off, but I recent learned that Roger fairly insisted upon studying medicine — it really is a passion for him."

"Doctor Larkin is a very good physician," Ellen agreed quickly, finding herself rather reluctant to continue on in the man's praises any further. Roger Larkin, with his handsome, but careworn face and gentle manner, had always seemed quite appealing to her, but as he had been attending her so closely of late, she felt a little embarrassed by the thought. No one, she thought, could blame her for wishing that he did not know just how foolish she had been. "I confess I *am* a little tired out from my visit, though, Mama. As you say, I didn't sleep well last night and think I ought to go lay down for just a little bit."

"Of course you ought to, dearest girl," Mrs. Millworth said, giving her one more squeeze before releasing her. "Rest as long as you are able. I will call you in plenty of time to dress for dinner."

Ellen stood.

"You know we must lie all of your woe at the feet of that blackguard," she said softly. "You mustn't blame yourself.

Ellen stiffened. Then she nodded as she left the sitting room and made her way to her own bedchamber. Of course, it was her fault, she thought. She was the one who encouraged him. If she had been a true lady, she never would have given the man the time of day once he started to pressure her for more intimacy. She had hoped to air her troubles to Arabella, but she could not cast a shadow on her friend's wedding, and her mother simply would not believe her child was anything but a victim in the assault.

Heaving a great sigh of relief once the bedroom door was closed behind her, Ellen allowed her false smile to fade. The room was still a bit unfamiliar. She had moved to a guest bedroom after her ordeal because she had been utterly incapable of sleeping in her childhood bedchamber. It was too great a reminder of the hours she had spent happily daydreaming over her erstwhile fiancé and his false, saccharine words. She had thought he loved her. Surely, she had loved him. How could she have been so taken in by his utter insincerity? How had she fallen prey to him, she wondered? She shoved the thought aside. It did not matter. It was in the past now. She must live in the present, and for the future.

THIS ROOM, SHE THOUGHT RATHER DREARILY, BORE NONE of those foolishly hopeful associations, only the strangely cold sense of despair that had enveloped her all autumn long. Sir James, or rather James Tyner, as his very name had been a lie, but she could never manage to think of him as anything besides Sir James was gone, and good riddance to him. Ellen could think fervently of his exile, but every bit as fervently did she mourn the loss of the man he had claimed and pretended to be, a gallant, sensitive gentleman with the soul of a poet and a heart filled with devotion and adoration for her and her alone. *That* loss was terrible indeed, although she realized now that she could not have lost that love, when it was never hers in the first place.

In the beginning, when their love was just a dear secret, and she had to content herself with his letters, she had easily idled away many afternoons just reading his beautiful words over and over again until they were imprinted upon her memory. It was a curse now, when she would have given anything to be rid of the nagging memories of his words. She wanted to forget, but it seemed she could not.

"My raven-haired goddess, I am fain to accomplish anything today as I cannot cease thinking of the perfection of your eyes, your laugh, your very essence. What a quandary I am in. It is the thorough resolution of my business affairs that keeps me wretchedly, miserably apart from your light, and yet I cannot give even the smallest portion of my mind to those matters for the idea of you reigns supremely over my mind. I have spent an hour or more already this morning attempting to wrench my attention to trivial, earthly responsibilities, but in vain. I have no responsibility greater than my duty to pay tribute to the queen of my heart with every breath, and I cannot persuade myself that to do otherwise is anything short of blasphemy. Heaven has seen fit to bless an undeserving wretch such as I with that most priceless of treasures, your regard, and surely, I must spend every moment paying tribute, my angel…"

CHAPTER 2

Ellen shook herself free of the memory. She could have recited pages of such intoxicating sentiment, like a child reciting a familiar prayer or a well-learned lesson. She had steeped herself in his adoration for most of the summer and then continued into autumn after Arabella and her family had come home from Bath. She had thrilled to the excitement of secretly corresponding with the handsome, attentive young gentleman who had professed his undying adoration of her from almost their first meeting. In hindsight, she could see, as everyone was so quick to assure her, that it was not so strange for a romantic, naïve girl to fall desperately in love when she was pursued so thoroughly.

When Sir James had returned to their sleepy little country village, his business affairs in order, and procured her father's blessing to take her hand, Ellen had been convinced she was the happiest girl in all of England. He seemed so utterly devoted to her, and quickly became her entire world. No one else, not her parents nor her oldest friend, seemed to exist as dim shadows in the background. His impatience with the preparations for the wedding was only further proof, as if she had needed any further indication of his great love, as was his intolerance for anyone other than himself occupying Ellen's time or attention.

Truly, he had taken command of nearly every thought and action that she had, his supremacy over her mind and heart almost perfectly complete. If he had been content to wait a few short weeks for their wedding date, Ellen had no doubt that she would still be under his thrall. It was only his fear of discovery that led him to overplay his hand and attempt to persuade her to run away with him.

Shuddering at the memory, Ellen recalled how close she had been to giving in to what had seemed a wildly romantic impulse. Sir James had miscalculated, however, in discrediting how strong a love she held for her parents. She was their only child and had received all of their tender love from the moment of her birth. Family was not only important to her parents, though. It was important to her. The idea of causing them pain by running away and creating a scandal had been unthinkable, even in the face of Sir James's most fervent and passionate declarations. She had to pause, and he would not allow her to do so. That was his undoing in the end. That and her good friend, Arabella.

The moment he'd realized she would not do his bidding was perhaps the worst moment of Ellen's life. He had grown furious and had changed his manner so suddenly and thoroughly that it was as if he had become another person before her very eyes. All charm and affection dropped away from him like a garment, and his eyes had become flat and cold. All pretense of gentle sensibilities drained away in an instant. That was the sight that haunted her nightmares so relentlessly. He had dragged her forcibly into his carriage and would have carried her away to disgrace, perhaps even an early grave, if it had not been for the heroic intervention of her dear friend, Lady Arabella Sedgewick and the lady's fiancé, Lord Willingham, Baron Wickingham.

It was thanks to their quick and determined actions that she had been returned safely home only hours later, reputation still intact. She surely would have been ruined without their intervention. Perhaps she would have been dead. A friend, even a single friend, with such undying faithfulness was such a blessing that a person could not consider that there should be more than one such devotee in one's life. Perhaps that was her mistake. She had thought Sir James Randall was as true and devoted as her dear friend, Arabella, and he was nothing the like.

Sir Randall had been revealed to be nothing more than a wily, desperate criminal, and was even now probably still on the vessel bound for the penal colony in Australia. The bottom of the earth was not a far enough distance, but it would have to do.

She ought to lie down and rest, as she had told her mother she would, but discontent made her restless and she paced the small room. It seemed to her that if she lay still, she would be instantly claimed and devoured by the rush of horrible emotions that dogged her every step lately. She could not sleep since there would come the nightmares, the price, she supposed, of nineteen years of carefree happiness, and of naïve, poor judgement. She *would* say it, at least to herself.

No matter how her parents and friends, and Doctor Larkin, for that matter, worked to impress upon her that Sir James had been a villain of monstrous cleverness who had fooled a great many older and wiser people, Ellen knew she still bore some blame in the recent disaster. She had been silly and too trusting. She had allowed the man to run roughshod over her without a peep of complaint. She had given over her autonomy, and although many women did subjugate themselves to men, especially their husbands, it was really a relief to acknowledge that she did have some control over her life.

Gazing at her reflection in the looking glass, Ellen was determined to face reality head on without the comforting gauze her affectionate connections insisted upon while attempting to shroud her from her present reality. Her pretty, pale rose gown hung a little loosely upon her frame, despite the fact her maid, Hortense, had taken it in only last week. Her complexion, once so glowing and creamy, looked dull, the dark shadows beneath her large blue eyes standing out in stark contrast to her waxlike pallor.

Even the silky masses of her ebony hair seemed lifeless and limp, despite the elegant way Hortense had pinned it up that morning. The darkness of her hair and eyes seemed to exaggerate the paleness of her skin. It was no wonder her mother and father were so horribly concerned for her well-being. She resembled a corpse, a wraith-like creature who was but a shadow of the woman she had once been, which was why Doctor Larkin continued to visit several times a week.

Slipping the pins from her hair, Ellen shook out the tresses as they fell over her shoulders. Sir James had once begged her for a lock of hair, and she had been all too glad to oblige him. She had cut it from the nape of her neck, and he had pressed it to his lips so fervently, like a man who had been granted a priceless treasure, his action thrilling Ellen to her very core. He would be hard-pressed to pretend such adoration now, she thought, running her fingers through her sad, lifeless locks. Or perhaps he wouldn't, since the man was an inveterate liar.

She had always been counted a beauty, but doubtlessly Sir James Randall would have professed her loveliness even if she had been a gorgon. It was her father's wealth he had desired, nothing more. Ah yes. He had been enamored all right, in love with her father's property and gold coins, not her. Still, she imagined he would scarcely recognize the pitiful, haunted-looking creature reflected in the looking glass. And once he *did* recognize her, he would have more than likely been pleased to have stolen her beauty along with her self-respect. The man would consider it turnabout and fair play since she had inadvertently cost him his freedom.

How ridiculous, Ellen thought, realization bursting upon her suddenly and shockingly. She *knew* Sir James to be the worst sort of dark-hearted villain. He had used her poorly and never even dreamed of loving her. Yet despite that knowledge, despite all the pain and suffering the man had caused, she was standing here imagining what he would think of her. Worse still, she found herself wishing for a chance to explain to Sir James that she had never meant to thwart his wretched plans. What a fool she was.

"If I were to stand before him this moment, I believe I would actually *apologize* to Sir James," she said aloud, shaken by the thought. "I would be unable to help myself. It is no wonder, out of all the heiresses he might have preyed upon, he set his sights upon me. I surely have the worst judgement and the most foolish heart of anyone who ever lived."

Suddenly furious with herself, Ellen snatched up a hairbrush and began to drag the brush through her hair with unaccustomed vigor. Sir James had been banished to the ends of the earth. Yet, the villain still managed to continually prey upon her mind, and worse, to hurt everyone who cared for her and already done so much to save her. It simply had to stop, she decided No more would she allow herself to indulgently waste away, drifting along upon waves of sadness. That was nothing, but yet another romantic folly, behaving like some sort of tragic Ophelia.

That woman let that mad wretch Hamlet decide her fate. How differently things might have gone if Ophelia had waded back out of the stream and put aside both her flowers and her feelings, Ellen thought. Yes, many women over the ages had allowed a man to rule over their lives. She vowed, at this very moment, she would be the master of her own life. She would not let her feelings dictate her actions. She would embrace new thoughts of rationality and logic. She would eschew her foolish emotions from this point forward.

"I shall be a new woman," she declared firmly, ringing for Hortense to come arrange her hair once more. "I have proven to myself, beyond any doubt ,that I cannot trust my heart or my emotions. I will not be guided by them for one moment more. If anything, I must attempt to do the very *opposite* of my feelings."

IN HIS DISORDERED AND RATHER DUSTY STUDY, DOCTOR Roger Larkin tossed aside the medical journal that he had been unsuccessfully attempting to read for the past quarter of an hour. That task had proved just as fruitless as the other abandoned attempts at work. He glanced at the clutter on his desk, notes of the diagnosis and treatment for various patients, a complicated surgical diagram, even a list of medical ingredients that he needed to order. None of it could hold his interest for more than a few moments, and Roger did not pretend that he did not know why.

His mind turned again and again to Miss Ellen Millworth, as it had done from the first day, when he had moved to the village to take up his medical practice alongside the elderly Dr. Harding. That dear woman was a distraction, once she had been a pleasant daydream, then a resigned sorrow when she was engaged to marry another. Recently, she had become an all-consuming distraction. Ever since she had been rescued from the clutches of that scoundrel, Randall, Ellen's enchanting, vivacious spirit had faded away to the point she was almost unrecognizable as the generous and laughing girl introduced to him. As her physician, Roger was plagued with concerns over the way her sorrow was destroying her health, turning her vivid beauty into a haunting, tragic loveliness. As a man, his feelings went much deeper. With a curse, he slapped the book closed as if its very words offended him. "Female hysteria indeed," he muttered, tossing the volume aside.

As the man who had been secretly and hopelessly in love with Miss Ellen Millworth upon first seeing her, he was tormented by the idea she might be beyond help or cure.

He wondered if Mrs. Millworth had remembered to insist that her daughter take the sleeping tincture he had delivered earlier. Peaceful, undisturbed sleep might do wonders for the woman, Roger knew. Sleep was the great healer. He also knew Mrs. Millworth would have been as diligent as himself in seeing that Ellen took the medicine. The real reason for his current distraction was that he had been counting on seeing Ellen that morning and had timed his visit poorly.

If he could have had but a moment with her, a chance to ascertain if her health had improved, perhaps make her smile, he would not now be so distracted. She was further beyond him than she had ever been, and Roger accepted that as fact. But he could never accept the fear that dogged him constantly, that her broken heart and shattered nerves might be beyond his ability to heal; that she might slip away from the world altogether. *That* would be unendurable.

With renewed resolve, he began leafing through the pages of the abandoned medical journal once more. Most of the treatises that he had found on broken hearts and melancholy were largely dismissive and useless. Others said that matters of the mind could not be cured and that the patient should be tucked away from polite society in some hell-hole like Bedlam. Of course, if the persons had enough money to spare, then a private hospital might be chosen. Even so, the solution was to hide the patient away from polite society. No cure was even hinted at.

He would not believe it. There must be something he could do. Surely *some* applicable research had been published. No one denied the idea that the mind could affect the health of the body, but all felt it was simply a matter of will. The strong-willed survived, and the weak-willed did not, and the female, as the weaker sex, began such things at a disadvantage, if he believed what he read.

He snorted with disgust. Did he believe this rot? Was his own mother weak-willed? Was Lady Arabella Sedgewick? The question was, was Miss Millworth? He could not accept it. He refused to. If there was one thing Roger believed in, it was his ability to find a way to heal

Ellen. Miss Millworth, he reminded himself. Yes, he would do his best to heal her and relieve her pains, even if he could never have her as his own. He would not give up on her. If she needed a strong will to survive, he would provide that will when she did not.

CHAPTER 3

The next day, Ellen was shown to Lady Arabella Sedgewick's solar, where her friend's maid, was putting the finishing touches on her coiffure.

"Ellen, what a happy surprise," Lady Arabella exclaimed delightedly, a brilliant smile lighting up her beautiful face at the sight of her friend. Always flawlessly lovely, Arabella had been transformed by love so much that she really seemed to glow with a tangible inner radiance of late. It was just what Ellen had always wanted for her oldest and dearest friend. Arabella's smile caused an answering expression to tug at her own lips. Perhaps, it was a smile that graced her face.

Arabella dismissed her maid with the admonition to have tea sent up while they waited until the others were ready to gather for the dinner party.

"I know, I said earlier that I doubted I would be able to come this evening," Ellen said, feeling a little sheepish despite the warmth of her welcome. "But I felt it might do me some good to get out of the house. Besides, it made poor Mama so happy to see me voluntarily taking an interest in something, I could not disappoint her."

"It makes me terribly happy as well, dearest," Arabella declared firmly, putting a hand on Ellen's arm as if to ensure she did not attempt to escape. "And really, in spite of my scrambling about to procure some entertainment for Father's last-minute guests, the music should be rather nice. It seems like it's been ages since we've heard anything new, and Miss Stanton is wonderfully talented."

"She is Lady Evans's niece, isn't she? I had heard that she came here recently to stay with her aunt, but I have not met her yet."

Truthfully, the thought of escape *had* crossed Ellen's mind. Recently, her narrow escape from matrimony had made her do her best to avoid most social situations. It was not merely that she felt self-conscious, although that was a foregone conclusion in their small and gossip-prone village. A near scandal such as hers was always a topic of intense scrutiny, and she doubted very much that the intervening months had lessened anyone's interest. Even a relatively informal gathering, such as tonight's small concert hosted by Lord Sedgewick, was certain to be riddled with curious stares and whispers. There would be numerous glances of speculation or questions she must either dodge or ignore, but she ordered herself to remain steadfast. Hadn't she just told her looking-glass she would not fade away like Ophelia and her summer flowers? No. She was made of stronger stuff than that.

"Yes, and Miss Stanton is a very pleasant lady. A bit plain, perhaps, but she surely possesses the patience of Job himself, for she never seems to mind Lady Evans and you know she can be a trifle demanding," replied Arabella with a laugh and a shake of her head at the understatement.

"A trifle," agreed Ellen, returning the smile. "But not nearly as demanding as Lady Mayberry." Lady Evans was a good hearted and generous woman, but notoriously opinionated, and her opinions were known to shift dramatically without warning.

"Will your Lord Willingham be dancing attendance?" Ellen asked, determined to make at least a pretense of feeling natural and at ease in the face of the various murmurs and glances that would follow her this evening. Fortunately, Arabella seemed to understand, as she always did.

"Unfortunately, no. He has returned to London for the purpose of buying a very particular horse for his stables, if you will believe me. He is determined, you know, to establish the finest line of thoroughbreds in all of England, and at the recommendation of one Mr. Richard Tattersall. He is certain that this particular horse must be included in his stable. I cannot say that I fail to understand why one particular stallion is *that* much better than another, especially another a little closer geographically. But he was positively delighted at the prospect the horse is for sale, and nothing could stop him from rushing off right away to this particular sale."

"But did you not wish to accompany him to Town?" Ellen inquired.

"Oh, no," Arabella laughed. "He has eyes only for his horses in such a state. I would likely be entirely forgotten."

"Surely, that is not so," Ellen exclaimed.

"No, but I do know when to allow him his delight," Arabella said. "Besides, he is bored to tears with talk of the wedding. I'm sure he would rather we had just moved on with it." Arabella laughed lightly and Ellen managed a genuine smile as the maid brought the tea.

"Shall I pour?" she asked.

"Oh, no, Delores. There must be a million things to get ready for tonight. We are fine here." Arabella reached out to pour, adding sugar and a dollop of cream to her friend's tea since she knew exactly how Ellen enjoyed the beverage.

"I must say, it is marvelous how Lord Willingham as restored those ruined old stables," Ellen replied as the two friends smiled at each other over their tea. "And even more marvelous that he is able to indulge in his passion now."

Arabella blushed and Ellen stammered her apology. "I mean the horses, of course," she said, her own face heating with embarrassment.

"Of course," Arabella agreed. "That is, in part, why I could not bring myself to protest his sudden trip to London, even though I *was* looking forward to his company for the rest of the week." She blew on her tea momentarily, then took a sip. "But not for the world could I have diminished his enthusiasm now that he is free to enjoy himself," Arabella said fondly. "After all, we have our whole lives before us." Arabella's eyes were alight with love.

Ellen felt a sudden rush of affection for Lord Christopher Willingham, although she really could not claim to know him well at all. However, anyone who could make Arabella so plainly happy would have Ellen's loyalty for life. Besides, that he had been instrumental in revealing the true nature of Sir James counted for a lot in Ellen's eyes. Only a few short months ago, Lord Willingham had inherited his uncle's title, along with an impressive collection of debts, a dilapidated farm near the village and a distinctly unsavory reputation. Ellen had been only marginally aware of him because that had been just around the time when Arabella's family had gone away to Bath, and Sir James had begun his relentless pursuit of her heart. It seemed everything had faded into the background at Sir James's onslaught of her body and soul. She shoved away the thoughts of Sir James, willing herself not to think of him at all.

The strong, rather reserved Lord Willingham had been ostracized by everyone in the neighborhood, owing to his uncle's reputation, and had largely kept to his impoverished farm, but that had all changed quite dramatically.

"I wish he had been able to come tonight, though," Ellen mused. "Really, I do not feel acquainted with Lord Willingham at all. Besides, I would dearly love to see how everyone has changed in their manner and treatment of him, now that his fortune has been restored, and he is to marry the most beautiful girl in all of England."

"I shall pretend to ignore that bit of flattery, of course," laughed Arabella. "It *is* rather funny to see the difference in society's acceptance of him, but it is annoying as well. He laughs at me because I still find myself feeling quite indignant about it. When I first returned from Bath, there was scarcely anyone in society here who would acknowledge poor Lord Willingham, and no one could say an actual reason for their hostile attitude. After all, it was never *his* fault that his uncle was a wastrel and a bit of a rake." Arabella waved a hand, brushing away the thoughts. "I dare not dwell on the subject, or I might become wrathful all over again."

"We would probably be wise to avoid that, then," Ellen said, casting about for an earlier topic of conversation. "You cannot deny that you are at least a little eager to see the stables at Willowbend restored and put to use for your own sake as well as Lord Willingham's. I always thought that you were more avidly fond of horses and riding than you cared to admit."

"That is true, I confess," laughed Arabella. "I was always afraid that if I ever indulged my unladylike taste for wild gallops, then the entire world might suspect I was not so decorous as I seemed."

Ellen chuckled, and Arabella paused the teacup at her lips. "It is good to see you smile," she said.

"Well, it is just that seeing you flying down the main thoroughfare last month has given your secret away, I am afraid. All the village knows how well you ride. You may as well indulge yourself from now on."

"That is just what my Lord Willingham said, but I-" Arabella broke off her words uncertainly, seemingly confused by Ellen's casual reference to that traumatic day.

"I am happily amazed," Arabella said.

"You would never have mentioned it, for fear of upsetting me, I know," Ellen said, drawing in a steadying breath. "I will not deny that it is a painful memory, but it is also a very fond one. You set aside so much that you held dear, risking a great deal without a single hesitation, to save me. You are a true friend. I am forever in your debt, and I will not be so ungrateful as to pretend that it did not happen."

"Ungrateful. Surely no one in the world could imagine applying such a term to you, dearest," protested Arabella.

"*I* can imagine it, and several other unflattering terms as well," returned Ellen steadily. "I have been rather ungrateful, and selfish as well, all but wrapping myself up in cotton wool and avoiding reality."

"Ellen, you have been subjected to a terrible shock," Arabella began, looking concerned. "It is understandable that you should take some time to recover."

"Have I been, though? I forced myself to take stock of everything yesterday. As far as I can tell, I am in a far worse condition now than I was at the end of the summer, through no one's fault but my own. You have all been lovely to indulge me, but I realized it is high time I stopped dwelling on my emotions - they are, after all, the very things that brought all this trouble to our families in the first place."

"It was that vile, reprehensible snake that brought trouble, not you," Arabella said, turning and grasping her friend's hands in solidarity. "Never you." For a moment, her friend's sounded so much like her mother, Ellen was taken aback. Perhaps that was how love spoke, never seeing flaws in the character of those they cared for.

"I let him in. I was so delighted to be wooed so perfectly that I was glad to turn a blind eye to a great many things. You cannot refuse me my share of the blame if you wish for me to truly recover."

"As a matter of fact," Arabella responded after a moment, "I believe I can refuse it if I so choose. You seem to have forgotten already, but you did just admit you are forever in my debt."

A true smile broke on Ellen's face. "That seems a particularly poor way to spend such a thing, if you ask me," Ellen found herself actually laughing as she looked into her friend's countenance. "Think of all the other things you might have demanded. Infinite possibilities, really, but far be it from me to criticize your choice or allow you to take it back now."

"There, I'm glad that's settled, then," Arabella laughed as well, and the intangible constraint that had lingered between them seemed to vanish in an instant. "You *do* look better tonight than you have lately. You are still far too thin and pale for my peace of mind, but stronger somehow."

"I slept well last night for the first time since Sir James made his attempt at stealing me away, and I really do think it is because I have made up my mind to stop trying to avoid addressing everything. I very likely could have gone on drifting lifelessly for a great deal longer, but I suddenly noticed how worn and tired poor Mama has become. I have put a great strain on her, and I cannot bear to go on causing her sorrow, now that I see she is suffering because of my melancholy."

"She has been terribly concerned, of course. We all have. But do not feel that you have to push yourself too far too quickly, Ellen," cautioned Arabella. "Your mother would never want that for you."

"Of course," Ellen murmured, knowing that any further argument would be in vain. "Now tell me, will Lord Willingham return in time for the hunting party next week?"

"He assured me that he would. I certainly hope he does, for he has a great deal to do here, overseeing all the work that is being done on poor old Willowbend Hall."

"Will it be ready in time for the wedding?" wondered Ellen doubtfully. It had been at least a month, she realized, since the last time she had seen the progress that was being made in restoring the old manor. It had been in such sad disrepair that she could scarcely imagine it being completed and fit for Arabella to preside over before the year was out.

"It doesn't have any other choice but to be ready," Arabella said with a touch of grim determination in her tone.

"Well, if anyone could order an inanimate pile of masonry to do her bidding through sheer force of will, I believe it would be you," Ellen said reassuringly.

Arabella nodded with her signature confidence and set the cup on the tray. "Shall we go down to see if any guests have arrived for the musicale?" she asked.

"Yes," Ellen said decisively. "We should."

Arm in arm, the two friends descended the stairs.

CHAPTER 4

After enduring the gauntlet of neighbors and acquaintances making polite small talk and thinly veiled curiosity, Ellen slipped away from Arabella's side to take a brief refuge in her favorite corner of the Sedgewick's familiar library. A sanctuary which *ought* to have been deserted. To her surprise and consternation, Doctor Larkin was already there, looking a trifle weary and rumpled as he always did. It was oddly appealing, somehow. Ellen thought fleetingly how startled the doctor would be if she turned the tables for once and ordered *him* to rest by the fireside with a cup of tea. A faint smile tugged at the corners of her lips as she surveyed him unnoticed. He had his back to her as he studied the books on the shelf.

His tailored navy-blue coat hugged his broad shoulders. The garment it was wrinkled, as if he had picked it up from a pile on a chair rather than the hand of an experienced valet. Truthfully, she didn't know if the man had a valet. Surely he did. His breeches, a pale doeskin, were fashionable and clean. They hugged his body quite enticingly. Oh bother, she thought. How dare she, a lady, notice such a thing?

He turned then, just noticing her in the doorway. "Miss Millworth," he said in surprise. A hand went to his silver and blue cravat, which he had obviously pulled loose from its tight knot. A moment later, his hand dropped from the accessory as he smiled at her. His smile lit up his face. She had always loved his smile. It seemed to bring joy from inside of her when there was no joy to be found. He was dressed as befitting his station this day rather than his profession. He was, after all, the grandson of a viscount, albeit on his mother's side.

He dropped his hand to the lapel of his dark blue jacket and took a step towards her. His waistcoat, beneath the jacket, a fine ivory wool, was in better repair than the wrinkled outer garment. It had a silver embroidered crest of the Larkin family, replete with leaves surrounding a peacock done in pale green thread as well as the silver which matched the silver buttons, a sign of his family's status and wealth, even though he had taken the path of a profession in the medical arts.

The garments fit his body snugly and added a touch of elegance and luxury that seemed unusual for the busy doctor.

"Oh, I did not realize anyone would be in here just now, please forgive my intrusion," she murmured, feeling a flush of embarrassment at her errant thought. She obviously should leave immediately, but she did not wish to do so.

"Not at all, Miss Millworth." He stepped forward and bowed formally over her hand. It seemed strange to see him socially when she normally greeted him from her bedside. She felt a blush color her face at the thought. She was not his patient now.

"I confess I only slipped in here a moment ago," he said. "I am ashamed to say with no purpose but to avoid a certain patient of mine, who *will* insist upon reciting a very lengthy list of completely imaginary symptoms. I am not usually such a coward, but it has been a trying sort of day, and I feared my face might give away certain unflattering opinions." Doctor Larkin said with an apologetic expression.

"I believe I can guess at the identity of that patient, and I may say that you ought to be perfectly safe now. I saw her closeting poor Mrs. Cooke only a moment ago, and you know she will not relinquish such a defenseless victim any time soon."

"Mrs. Cooke's sacrifice does not go unappreciated," responded the doctor fervently, casting his eyes heavenward as he straightened his jacket over his embroidered waistcoat. He paused with his hand held over the last silver button. "Your mother mentioned earlier to me that I might see you here this evening. She was quite delighted you felt well enough to attend, as a matter of fact." The doctor moved towards the door and Ellen was quite aware that to be found in this moment of privacy with the doctor could be construed as scandalous, but she was unwilling to give up the moment just yet. Besides, it was a small party consisting mostly of the Sedgewicks and their close friends.

"That is more than half of the reason that I ordered myself to leave the house," Ellen replied frankly. She did not add that the other half of the reason, perhaps more than half, was to see Doctor Larkin himself. "As fond as I am of music, even the draw of hearing such an accomplished harpist as Miss Henley is not more powerful than my newfound resolution to boost my mother's spirits."

"That is certainly an admirable resolve. I wonder if I might be so bold as to inquire what prompted it?" asked Doctor Larkin curiously, studying Ellen with what she thought of as his physician's gaze. It was a sort of intense scrutiny and assessment that was surely measuring and noting any number of outward signs of health. Well, she thought, there was that. If found in this moment of private conversation, no one would give them a second thought, least of all the doctor himself. After all, he saw her as nothing more than a patient.

"Oh, any number of things," Ellen said with an attempt at an airy and unconcerned manner. Perhaps if she purported herself in a bright and fetching way, he might notice more about her than her illness. "I find myself growing quite weary of moping about and thinking only of myself, for one. But more importantly, I noticed recently, and I daresay it has not escaped your notice, either, that Mama seems quite exhausted and careworn. I am the reason for that, and I mean to be the reason for her improvement as well." Ellen lifted her chin with determination.

"You must not place such a burden of blame upon yourself, Miss Millworth," the doctor began earnestly, but Ellen silenced him with a look.

"Doctor Larkin, as a physician, you cannot mean to tell me that you think my mother is in the best of health at the moment?" She placed her hands on her hips and raised an eyebrow.

"I do not say that," he admitted, frowning a little.

"And furthermore, you cannot claim that her great concern for me is not at the root of her weariness," she continued on ruthlessly before he could begin to argue. "It seems an obvious conclusion then, that if she were not so laden with anxiety on my behalf, she would begin to improve, is that not so?"

"That is a rather black and white view of the matter," Doctor Larkin complained ruefully. "Medicine is never so exact, but I cannot disagree with your assessment, on the surface, at least. I would beseech you, however, to not take on too great a burden of self-recrimination, and to not overexert yourself too much. No one, least of all your mother in my opinion, begrudges you the time and care that your recovery has required. It would be unfortunate indeed if your well-intentioned resolution caused a relapse. I am certain that nothing would distress Mrs. Millworth more than such an event."

"That is a clever way of putting it, Doctor Larkin," Ellen said with a little laugh, smiling up at him. "Turning everything about in such a manner. Are all physicians so well versed in the art of persuasion?"

"Seeing as I spend a great deal of my time convincing my patients to follow my orders, it really ought to have been a part of my medical training, but I must confess that instead, that particular skill of mine was honed in childhood, out of sheer necessity owing the great number of brothers that I possess."

"That would certainly necessitate such a talent," Ellen agreed, her smile deepening so that the dimples in her cheeks winked into being for the first time in a great many weeks. "I had forgotten, but of course I *did* know that you hail from a very large family. How many are there?"

"Five boys and three girls still living," Doctor Larkin answered, a little distractedly. "And I rank squarely in the middle, so I am quite familiar with the role of negotiator. I hope that I have managed to use my small talent in that area to persuade you to embrace moderation as you resume more of your usual activities?"

"You have, I confess. Particularly since you have not done me the discourtesy of denying my assertions, but also because I *did* find myself in need of a brief refuge after only a quarter of an hour of polite company."

"A great many people find polite company to be rather overtaxing even when they are in the best of health, particularly when it involves such an amount of curiosity and speculation. Besides, a quarter of an hour is quite a long time after a period of illness, you know. But you are in danger of missing the music."

"Not to mention the fact that if I disappear for very long, I will simply be inviting more curiosity and speculation," Ellen agreed, finding herself strangely reluctant to end their conversation, nevertheless.

"There is that," the doctor said with a wry expression, offering his arm gallantly to her. "Shall I escort you back?"

"I do not think that would do," she answered. "There may be talk."

"Talk?" he repeated blankly.

She looked askance. "Was it possible that she was so beneath his notice as a woman that he did not realize how the gossips would run with the news of their private moment in the library?"

"Oh. Yes. Of course," he said belatedly, his ears coloring with a faint tinge of red.

Ellen took the doctor's arm, allowing herself to feel supported momentarily by his reassuring presence. There was something so irresistibly dear about Doctor Larkin, she thought yet again. He was so unfailingly gentle and steady, and the fact he spent all of his time caring for his fellow man and very little on his own personal comfort made Ellen long to straighten his cravat, or urge him to eat a proper meal, or scold his valet for allowing his coat to be in such a state of perpetual shabbiness.

"Thank you. All appearances aside, I *do* want to hear the music." She sighed. "However, we should probably re-enter the room separately."

"Oh course," he repeated.

Glancing up, she saw he was smiling down at her in a way that transformed his weary face into something startlingly handsome, his steely grey-blue eyes filled with such intelligence and compassion despite the shadows beneath them. Her heart suddenly racing, Ellen glanced away quickly in confusion. Why, she was thinking of him romantically she realized, heat rushing to her face. It was mortifying, to think she would fall for the first person to offer her a bit of compassion, for that was all it was on the doctor's part, she was sure. He was a caring person who treated all of his patients with regard. Thank goodness the man could not read her thoughts, in spite of his keen perception.

He would be hard pressed not to laugh in her face if he had any notion of what was in her mind, Ellen was certain, despite his unfailing kindness. She was nothing more than a silly little fool, and he knew that fact far more fully than most, in distressing detail. Well, she thought, carefully composing her expression and making sure that she looked anywhere but in the doctor's direction, she could not have found better confirmation if she had searched for a year. Clearly, her heart was determined to make an ever-greater fool of her. It was not to be trusted for an instant.

"Oh, excuse me, Doctor," she said in a decidedly cool and distant tone as the first notes of the harp floated out of the conservatory doors. It would never do to remain in his company another moment longer. No doubt he was perceptive enough to notice her agitation and clever enough to discern the reason for it. Aside from how humiliating she would find his pity, Ellen would hate to cause him any discomfort, and surely the knowledge of her ridiculous sensibilities would accomplish just that. "I see Marianne and wanted particularly to ask her something."

"Of course, Miss Millworth," Doctor Larkin responded politely, bowing to her with renewed formality and stepping back. She took her leave of him without another word, leaving him to watch her with a secretly aching heart. He looked after her for a long moment. Why had he not kissed her? He chided himself.

CHAPTER 5

Ellen sat down to her breakfast the next morning with a better appetite than she could remember having in weeks. It took only one quick, surreptitious glance at her mother to see that her enthusiasm for the meal was both noticed and appreciated.

"Did you have a nice time last night, darling?" Mrs. Millworth asked hopefully, cutting into her own breakfast with an air of renewed enthusiasm. "I was so pleased that you decided to go, even though your father and I were unable to attend."

"I certainly did, Mama. I do hope your megrim is better."

"Oh, it is. It is," she assured her daughter. "Tell me about the music."

"Well, of course, Arabella counted herself fortunate that Miss Stanton was able to play at such short notice. She is quite talented and played ever so many new songs. You ought to have seen little Daphne, she was so entranced by the music that she was more still than I would have dreamed possible."

"I imagine that Miss Stanton was more than happy to oblige Arabella, and to take a few hours respite from her aunt in the bargain."

"As for little Daphne," Ellen added, "she is fourteen. Hardly a child any longer."

"Yes, but she certainly has been coming along nicely ever since the earl realized he needed to take a more active interest in his daughters," agreed Mrs. Millworth with a smile of satisfaction. "I must say I have always had a soft spot for Daphne Sedgewick. She is such a headstrong child. She reminds me of my self at that age."

"Mama, you were never so wild as young Daphne," Ellen argued dryly. "I don't believe it for an instant."

"I suppose not," Mrs. Millworth agreed. "I learned at a young age to bridle such passion, except for your father." She winked at her daughter, and Ellen stared aghast.

"Mama."

"Oh, I just want you to know that passions are not necessarily a bad thing, dear daughter."

Ellen nodded although she was not sure she agreed. She assumed that her mother was making an oblique reference to her ill-fated and mercifully brief engagement. If so, passion was certainly a bad thing.

"It was your father, you know, who suggested that the earl find a regular music instructor for Daphne," Mrs. Millworth continued. "But I daresay he had no idea it would be so successful. Daphne has inherited her mother's talent for music, which I always thought was something special, and the discipline of developing that talent seems to have been rather transformational."

"It is a weight off of Arabella's mind, I am sure," Ellen mused with a slight frown. "She has said as little to me, doubtless not wishing to distress me with her own worries. But I know her concern for Daphne's behavior and her future prospects must be rather heightened as her wedding day draws nearer. After all, once Arabella is married, she will not be so constantly on the spot to manage the girl."

"Ah well, these things have a way of working themselves out, you know," Mrs. Millworth observed comfortably. "And besides that, Daphne will always be very thoroughly herself no matter how much polish she does or does not gain."

"That's true enough, but she *did* follow poor Miss Stanton around most persistently after the conclusion of the music, demanding to be shown some specific technique or other," laughed Ellen as she recalled the rather harried look on the harpist's plain but pleasant face. "Where is Papa, by the way? I thought I was up early enough to eat breakfast with you both this morning."

"Oh, the poor man has not had so much as a bite of his breakfast. He was called away terribly early by one of the overseers, something about a problem with the livestock, I believe."

"I wouldn't have thought there could be anything particularly urgent with livestock, but then I suppose I know very little about such things."

"I cannot claim much more knowledge myself," admitted Mrs. Millworth, a little line of distress creasing her brow. "But in this case, I am afraid it might be rather serious. I hadn't mentioned it before, for fear of upsetting you further, my love, but there has been something of a rash of dead cattle and sheep around the village lately. I must say, I feel for the Duke of Brambleton. He only just seen the town of Northwick through last winter with the influenza, and then the flooding and poor crops. I wonder how much more our little town can take."

"I'm sure it was Dr. Harding and Dr. Larkin who saw the town through the influenza, not the duke," Ellen said.

"Of course, but the dying livestock must still concern the nobility."

"No more than the rest of us," Ellen said. "I do believe I heard some talk of it last night."

"Truly?" Mama asked.

Ellen shook her head. "Not a conversation that I was having, but just fragments of other people's conversations that one can't help but overhear, you know. I didn't really pay much attention at the time. I was more interested in the music." And grateful that people were discussing something other than her still-recent escapade, she added mentally.

"Nearly all the larger estates in this area have experienced some losses, from what I understand, but no one seems to know what is causing the animals to die. It's really quite disturbing... but you mustn't let it upset you, of course, darling. I could shake myself for saying anything. It was terribly thoughtless of me, and just when you're starting to get a bit of color and appetite back," Mrs. Millworth concluded, looking contrite.

"Don't be silly, Mama, it won't do me a bit of harm to think of some problems other than my own for a change. You cannot keep me sheltered from every bit of unpleasantness any longer, you know."

"Why, I most certainly *can*. You need to be sheltered, Ellen, until you are strong enough--"

"Which I will most likely never be if you insist upon treating me like an invalid forever," Ellen pointed out gently, recalling Doctor Larkin's trick of persuasion and employing it ruthlessly. "Just like I would never have learned to walk as a baby if you had insisted upon carrying me everywhere all the time."

"You are jesting, but as a matter of fact I really did want to keep you in my arms forever," admitted Mrs. Millworth with a quick laugh at the memory. "Your father used to tease me so terribly about just that. But he could hardly blame me, really, you were just the sweetest, most charming infant who ever existed. It is a wonder your wee little feet ever touched the ground. Everyone doted upon you so."

"Come to think of it, I believe that quite a few of my earliest memories were of being held and carried. I suppose that hardly anyone is so fortunate as I have been, in feeling so perfectly loved and cherished as far back as they can recall."

"Your father and I *have* always loved and cherished you, so much, you know. Oh, there you are, John." Mrs. Millworth exclaimed distractedly, mid-sentence as her husband entered the dining room. "Sit down, my dear, you must be quite famished by now." Her mother rang for the footman to bring more hot tea and breakfast for her husband.

"I am afraid I have little of an appetite at all," Mr. Millworth replied, taking his seat rather heavily. He looked distinctly upset; Ellen realized with concern as she hastened to pour him some tea.

"Was it something wrong with the sheep, Papa?" she asked, and he started a bit, as if surprised to see her at the table.

"Oh, I don't want you to fret, my dear," he said, casting a quick glance at his wife as he spoke. "It is no matter."

"I was just telling Ellen about the trouble that has been going around lately," Mrs. Millworth said before Ellen could voice her protest at being shut out. "She heard some talk of it at the concert at the Sedgewick's last night, you know."

Something in her voice and manner seemed to signal to Mr. Millworth that he need not entirely conceal his distress, and his shoulders sagged a bit. There was more gray at his temples than Ellen had noticed in the past, she realized. He was looking very nearly as careworn as his wife. When had her parents become old, she wondered. A wave of guilt and self-recrimination rose up within her, but was almost instantly matched, then washed away with another wave of a less familiar feeling. It was a sensation of wrath directed at Sir Randall for bringing so much trouble to so many people, although she could not blame the man for sick livestock.

In all the time since he had deceived her; in the time that he was only interested in her because it served his base, mercenary desires; in all the time during his attempted kidnapping of her and his ill treatment of her, Ellen had never quite worked up any true anger for the scoundrel. She had felt numb. Now, the anger erupted. The feeling was both alarming and liberating, and she had to work hard to set it aside enough to focus on what her father was saying.

"It seems to be the same sort of thing, I am afraid. A little more than fifty sheep, all unmarked and unharmed as far as anyone can tell, aside from the fact that they are dead. It is a terrible waste, and of course Edwards, who was in charge of the flock, feels dreadful. The man blames himself. He actually thought I would dismiss him, as if anyone would think this was his fault." Mr. Millworth shook his head, then took a sip of his tea absentmindedly.

Edwards must have been distraught indeed, Ellen considered, to entertain such a notion. Mr. Millworth had a great reputation as one of the most generous and considerate members of the landed gentry, and was unfailingly fair in all of his dealings with those who depended upon him.

"Why of course you would never dismiss Edwards," Mrs. Millworth averred, looking horrified at the very notion. "He has always been a steadfast worker for many years. And besides that, he and his wife have that poor, ailing little boy of theirs, who needs such particular care. You could never be so callous and unfeeling as to turn them out of their home at such a time."

"Oh, Mama, I had forgotten all about Thomas," exclaimed Ellen, stricken at the realization. Their tenant's youngest son was a sweet, bright little boy of six years who had struggled mightily to recover from the influenza the previous year, and Ellen had always doted upon him especially. "How perfectly beastly I have been, not even sparing him a thought in so long when I always used to visit him so often. I suppose I've been so caught up in my own affairs. How is he coming along?"

"A little better some days, his mother says, but she fears he will never be truly strong and well again. He has asked after you several times. I believe he is worried you have been unwell yourself. Doctor Larkin could give you a more thorough report, I daresay, for he checks in on the child often and will never hear of taking any payment from Edwards. He says he is only in need a cup of tea half-way through his rounds."

"Well, you may ask the doctor presently if you wish," Mr. Millworth interjected, and Ellen looked up suddenly. The words sent a jolt thorough her nerves.

"I sent Edwards along to fetch him," her father continued, "And so, unless he is out attending upon someone else at this hour, he will doubtless be along quite soon."

"Are you quite alright?" Mrs. Millworth asked her daughter.

"I'm fine, Mama," Ellen said hastily.

"You look a little flushed." She laid a hand on her daughter's forehead, checking for fever as she turned to her husband. "Why ever did you send for the doctor?" asked Mrs. Millworth.

"Because I cannot make any sense of this trouble with the sheep, to say nothing of the cattle down the lane earlier in the week and all the other unexplained livestock deaths," Papa answered rather tersely, and there was an unmistakable sign of anger in his usually patient expression. "No one has been able to come up with an answer, and for some reason they all seem contented enough to simply shrug at the loss. But it doesn't sit right with me, not by half. I believe I shall be unable to set the matter aside if I have not at least attempted to discover the cause."

"And you think that Doctor Larkin will be able to discover it?" Ellen wondered, a trifle doubtfully.

"Doctor Larkin is more than a simple country physician, my dear," her father said reprovingly. "Although he is certainly greatly skilled in his chosen profession. He has perhaps one of the greatest scientific minds of his generation. It is considered in some circles to be rather a loss that he has chosen to pursue practical medicine rather than the more experimental and intellectual sciences. It is rather ridiculous, I will grant you, for me to ask such a mind to examine mere livestock, but I have no doubt that he will be able to ascertain the problem, and he will not think such a task beneath him, either."

"I had no idea," murmured Ellen. It did not surprise her that her father had discovered so much about the doctor, for while Mr. Millworth was not particularly interested in scientific advancements and other intellectual pursuits Papa *was* deeply fascinated by the lives and experiences of his fellow man.

"He is such a *kind* man," Mrs. Millworth added complacently. "Second only to you my dear John. I know his family a little. His mother and I came out at the same Season, actually."

"His mother had a Season?" Ellen inquired.

"Oh yes. She was after all the daughter of a viscount." Mama shook her head. "Her parents were quite put out, you know. She was contracted to marry a duke, but love will have its way. We have always corresponded, and I recall the letters she used to write to me when her children were young. There was always some heartwarming little anecdote of her husband's gentleness and compassion and her sons who became such upright young gentlemen. Some men are just born good, I believe, and continue on that way."

And some men were just born wicked, Ellen reflected, letting her mother's continued praise of Roger Larkin flow unheeded as her own thoughts returned to Sir James Randall. She never could get out of the habit of referring to him by his false name and title, no matter how hard she tried. Again, the deep and burning feeling cascaded over her. She did not like the unfamiliar sensation of anger that welled up within her. No, it was not simple anger. It was rage. She tamped it down mercilessly. A lady should not feel such things.

CHAPTER 6

"I am glad that you sent for me," Doctor Larkin spoke a little absently as he matched his stride to that of Mr. Millworth. The two men made their way quickly through the late harvested pasture, the chilly wind whipping at them. "I will confess that I have been rather tormented by curiosity regarding this recent crop of trouble hereabouts."

"Ah, and here I was feeling decidedly foolish to impose on your time for such a trivial matter," Mr. Millworth remarked with a short laugh. "But as I was telling my wife and daughter before you arrived, there isn't another man in this part of the country with a sharper intellect than yours, and I am more than a little disturbed by these… occurrences, I suppose I should term them. These were fine, healthy sheep, and did not deserve such destruction."

"I absolutely agree with you," said Doctor Larkin firmly, seeing that his companion looked rather embarrassed to be admitting such a sentiment aloud. "I would not have devoted myself to the profession of medicine if I did not find the unnecessary loss of life—all life—to be abhorrent."

"Yes, that is just what I meant," Mr. Millworth said with a tone of relief. "Here they are; you see. Not a mark on them, no sign of a struggle or anything of that sort. I cannot imagine what sort of event would fell over fifty healthy animals at once, and yet that is just what seems to have happened here. It is a mystery."

"Just as at the other estates," the doctor murmured, kneeling beside the nearest wooly corpse with no regard whatsoever for the well-being of his trousers. He made a thorough examination before moving on to several other sheep in turn.

At length, he turned to Mr. Millworth, who had been joined once more by Edwards. The man was hanging back quietly during the examination unwilling to interrupt his betters.

"I wonder if you might have one of these ewes delivered to my house?" the doctor said at last. "I realize it sounds rather an odd thing to request, but there are some tests I should like to perform, and I can hardly carry the necessary equipment and chemical compounds all the way through these pastures, or at least, not easily."

"Yes, certainly, anything you need. Edwards will arrange for that right away, won't you, Edwards?"

"Aye," agreed the sturdy, ruddy-faced tenant, his brow still creased with anxiety and distress. "Have you any idea what has happened to them, sir?"

"I have several ideas, but I hardly like to speculate until I can be more certain. I will say right out this is quite concerning."

"I am grateful to you, Doctor Larkin, for taking the matter so seriously," Mr. Millworth said as Edwards moved to heft one of the unfortunate ewes into a wheelbarrow. "And at the same time, I find myself wishing, rather unreasonably, I daresay, that you did not find that it merited your concern."

"We must postpone our worry, sir, until I can provide some more clarity," the doctor said soothingly. Aside from the enduring strength of his feelings for Ellen Millworth, Roger had always liked her father for his own sake, appreciating the gentleman's forthrightness and humanity. "Perhaps you will be so good as to give my regrets to Mrs. Millworth. I know she had wanted me to stop and come in for a moment or two once we finished out here, but I really think I had better get to work on this immediately. The sooner we have answers, the sooner we will know what, if anything, needs to be done."

Mr. Millworth was predictably agreeable, and the doctor took his leave rapidly, still sparing a fleeting backward glance at the lovely home that was graced by Ellen. He allowed himself a moment to acknowledge the vise-like longing that clenched his heart mercilessly every time he was near her, but continued on his way with barely a hitch in his stride. She was safe and her health seemed to finally be improving along with her spirits, but he could not ignore the cold fear he felt at the idea of death coming so close to her home, even if it was only the death of an ewe.

Probably. Hopefully, his initial assessment was wrong, but Roger Larkin knew himself well enough to know that he would be unable to rest until the puzzle were resolved, particularly if doing so might ensure Ellen's continued well-being.

LATER IN THE DAY, WHEN THE SUN WAS ALREADY beginning to drift slowly towards the horizon, Ellen stood arm in arm with Arabella in the courtyard of the Millworth estate, admiring the glossy-flanked stallion that Lord Willingham had returned with so triumphantly.

"He is truly a magnificent creature," Ellen said honestly, smiling at the boyish delight that was so clearly evident in Lord Willingham's manner. It was not too long ago that he had been quiet and reserved to the point of seeming surly, which had not helped improve his estimation in the eyes of the village. She would scarcely have recognized him as the man laughing down at Arabella from his spirited new mount.

"He will be the pride of my stables, I am certain," agreed Lord Willingham with a quick smile for her as he dismounted with an easy grace that belied his stature.

"He already has my fullest admiration, although I suspect he must have wings hidden about somewhere. I can scarcely believe how quickly you made the return journey, and yet he appears perfectly well-rested already," Arabella declared.

"You may put him through his paces soon enough, and find out for yourself," promised her fiancée. "But regardless, he will require a more imaginative name than Pegasus."

"Daphne would all but disown me, I daresay," laughed Arabella. "But I warn you, she is most unpredictable when it comes to bestowing names on animals. You mustn't let her wheedle you into letting her name the pride of your stables."

"Remember when she christened an entire litter of kittens after her favorite apostles?" recalled Ellen with a laugh of her own. "We were certain that the vicar was going to die of horror when the tale was carried to him, but when he came to call…"

"Ostensibly to appeal to Daphne's better nature," Arabella put in merrily, "I still think the poor man half suspected her of being some sort of changeling."

"He might have," Ellen agreed, secretly delighted by the interruption, as she and Arabella had always been in the habit of telling stories in tandem and she had missed that simple yet unmistakable sign of their renewed harmony. "He is a funny, old-fashioned sort of vicar and he always took superstitions and things rather to heart although I suppose he has mellowed somewhat since the Duke of Brambleton rocked the parish with his wedding."

Lord Willingham frowned. "What on earth scandal could a duke cause?"

"You have no idea," Arabella laughed.

"In any case," Ellen continued, "I am surprised the man did not recommend burning Daphne at the stake or some such precaution."

"It did not help that the entire litter was black," Arabella added.

"I can easily imagine Daphne inventing some incantations or potions on the spot merely for the sake of frightening the man," Lord Willingham exclaimed, obviously enjoying the story greatly.

"She certainly would have done so if it had occurred to her, but happily it did not," Arabella gave a little shudder at the idea. She too could picture such a scenario quite clearly.

"We still don't quite know *exactly* what she did say to the vicar. Whatever it was, he actually ended up taking the Apostle John home with him to the vicarage, where he was by all accounts a great comfort to the vicar."

"And caught the mice at the parsonage," Ellen concluded the story, smiling companionably at Lord Willingham. It was odd, but she found herself quite comfortable in his company, for his own sake as well as because he made Arabella so happy.

"I ought to have guessed it would be something like that now that I think of it. Is your family expecting a visitor, Miss Millworth?" Lord Willingham added, still laughing as he gestured towards the lane where a horse and rider had just appeared.

"Not to my knowledge," Ellen said doubtfully, "and I cannot imagine who might be coming here in such frightful haste."

"Why, it's Doctor Larkin," exclaimed Arabella as the rider galloped closer into view. "I hope no one is ill."

"Perhaps he has some news regarding the dying livestock, I know Papa asked him to examine the sheep this morning and see if he could determine what had killed them."

"What's that, now?" Lord Willingham asked curiously. "Your family hasn't suffered the same trouble that has been going around, has it Miss Millworth? I got home quite late last night and have been busy settling this fine fellow into his new home today."

"I hadn't heard either," added Arabella, her expression growing more concerned. "I have spent the day closeted with my dressmaker and have not heard any news."

"It slipped my mind," Ellen admitted. "Edwards found a great many of our flock dead this morning, it is really quite dreadful. I didn't know until then that such a thing had been happening lately. Mama has been so careful to keep any upsetting news away from me, I did not hear of the trouble until today."

CHAPTER 7

"Hello there, Doctor," Lord Willingham hailed the gentleman as he drew near to the group in the courtyard looking tense and harried. "Is everything alright?"

"Good afternoon. And no, not precisely, I fear," Doctor Larkin answered grimly. Even the sight of Ellen interacting with friends, a healthy color blooming in her cheeks and an animated spark of interest in her lovely eyes, did not bring a smile to his face although his expression did soften by several degrees. "Is your father at home, Miss Millworth?"

"Yes, he has been shut up in his study for the better part of the day," Ellen said, feeling a chill creep over her. The autumn afternoon sun was still bright, and the day had warmed considerably since that morning, but she shivered suddenly and naturally Doctor Larkin noticed.

"That wrap is not really thick enough to keep you warm, Miss Millworth, and you ought not risk catching a chill," he reprimanded gently as he dismounted and passed his horse off to a waiting groom. For a brief instant he laid a testing hand on her arm, then frowned. "You *are* too cold to be standing out here. It is healthy to take the air, but please do wear your woolen wrap."

"I haven't been out long. Lady Arabella and Lord Willingham just stopped by a few minutes ago so I could see the new horse," Ellen explained, ignoring the thrill that ran up her arm at his touch.

Doctor Larkin only nodded at this statement, apparently blind to the majesty of the stallion as his attention was fixed on speaking with Mr. Millworth, but then suddenly his eyes sharpened, and he turned to Lord Willingham.

"Lord Willingham, you now own considerable land in this area, unless I am mistaken?"

"That is correct," assented the other man with a puzzled expression. Lord Willingham had only recently acquired much of his holding, for he had been unable to make any addition to the small farm he had inherited until he recovered the bulk of his wealth from Sir Randall.

"Have you much livestock, sir?"

"A fair amount, although I would not say that the property is being used to its full potential yet."

"Then, I think perhaps you will wish to hear what I have to say to Mr. Millworth, as well," Doctor Larkin said, his expression more grim than ever. "I believe it concerns all the landowners hereabouts."

The four went quickly inside the Millworth home, Ellen and Arabella trailing a few steps behind the men in an attempt to remain unobtrusive. Their presence was evidently all but forgotten in the face of whatever crisis Doctor Larkin had uncovered, and both knew that the best way to hear the news in such a case was to avoid notice.

They need not have worried, however, for both Mr. and Mrs. Millworth were right at hand and Doctor Larkin evidently felt that his news was rather too urgent to wait upon formalities.

"Mr. Millworth, I came as quickly as I could. It is very fortunate indeed that you sent for me to examine the animals this morning," he declared. "I have concluded my examination and performed several tests, and I would swear to it that the flock has been deliberately poisoned."

"Deliberately, you say? Who on earth would do such an abominable thing?" Mr. Millworth exclaimed, aghast.

"And *why*?" added in Mrs. Millworth.

"That is very bad news indeed," Lord Willingham said, his tone calmer and more speculative, but Ellen noticed he had, perhaps unconsciously, taken a step or two closer to Arabella, as if to guard her from some attack. "But hardly the reason that you rode over here in such a terrible haste, I should imagine. Such findings could easily have been communicated by way of a note or an assistant unless there is some immediate danger."

"You are correct in your assessment, sir," agreed the doctor, even as Mrs. Millworth blanched and looked faint. "It is very likely that there is no threat to human life here, but I could not risk a delay without absolute certainty. It is imperative that we discover just exactly how the poison was introduced into the systems of the animals."

"Do you mean to say that it might be something that could also poison the household?" asked Arabella, her eyes widening in alarm.

Ellen, seeing that her mother was trembling and pale, left the questioning to the others and led Mrs. Millworth to a seat.

"It is not impossible," Doctor Larkin was saying. "But as there was no loss of human life where the other incidents occurred. I am most likely alarming everyone unduly. Still, I think we had better search to see if we can find the source of the toxin. In the meantime, I think it will be best if the wells are checked and no one eats any meat which might be tainted, just as a precaution. We should send word to the others who have lost livestock."

"And send for the magistrate as well," added Lord Willingham, and Ellen could see that all the boyish happiness in his eyes had been replaced with something fierce and deadly. "Whoever has done this must be stopped as quickly as possible and made to answer for their crimes."

The men galvanized into action immediately, and Mrs. Millworth quickly recovered her presence of mind. She was distinctly concerned and yet she rallied. She called for the housekeeper to alert her of the situation and ensure that none of the servants partook of any food or drink until the danger had passed.

"If worse comes to worst, I suppose we shall have to send to the inn and see if they can provide an evening meal for the staff," she said briskly, no trace of upset to be found.

Both of her parents had such remarkable strength of character, Ellen reflected as she, Arabella, and Mrs. Millworth settled into the parlor to wait. Her parents were understandably upset and yet they rose splendidly to even the worst of occasions. They were extraordinarily gentle people, so much so that it was easy to assume they might fall to pieces in a crisis, as Ellen herself had done, and yet, they rose to meet the threat with vigor. Lord Willingham, too went from affable to dangerous in the space of mere moments. And she had never before seen Doctor Larkin look so grim and single-minded. Dreadful events such as this revealed a great deal about a person's verve, she supposed.

As she settled in with her needlepoint, Ellen considered Dr. Larkin's comments. It surely did not mean anything significant, that in spite of everything else, the doctor had been concerned that she might take a chill, Ellen told herself sternly. It would be foolish to read anything into that. He was a doctor after all, simply looking after the well-being of his patient. It was foolish to consider that he saw her as any more than one more sick person to cure; it was still more foolish that she felt warmed at the recollection of the simple interaction, but she could feel the sensation of his hand on her arm as vividly as if it had only just happened. Oh, she was too romantic by half. She had been so taken in my Sir Randall, and now, she read some romantic tendencies into the barest concern. Still, the thought that the doctor may care for her brought a warm feeling to her bosom.

CHAPTER 8

The time spent waiting seemed interminable to Ellen, despite being in the company of two of her favorite people. Mrs. Millworth and Arabella were both as tense as she was herself, and although they made an effort to discuss more amiable topics, it was impossible to refrain from speculating as they busied themselves with their needlework. It seemed strange to not have a cup of tea to sip, but until Dr. Larkin determined that the water was not tainted, he suggested no food or drink be consumed.

"No one in the village could be capable of doing such a wicked thing," Mrs. Millworth averred stoutly. "It must be the work of some sort of deranged, wandering lunatic, I think."

"If that is so, then I rather wish they would *keep* wandering. This has been going on for more than a fortnight. It seems that someone would have noticed a deranged stranger in that length of time," Arabella pointed out.

"A person does not necessarily have to be a lunatic to be wicked," mused Ellen softly, thinking of Sir James once more. *He* had been perfectly sane, she was certain. He simply found enjoyment in deceit and inflicting pain. "And I am not confident that any of us can ever say what people are or are not capable of, not even people we think we know quite well, or those we think we know well. In truth, one never really does know another human being, I think. One cannot be sure." She broke off embarrassed by her outburst.

"Oh, dearest, I did not mean to make you think of…" began Mrs. Millworth, wincing at her choice of words.

"Of course, you didn't, Mama," Ellen gave her mother a reassuring smile. "But I have learned a few lessons from my recent trials, or at least, I certainly hope that I have. That is merely one of them. Things are not always as they seem. People are not always as they seem. Even those that you think love you, can be deceptive."

"I believe you are right," said Arabella contemplatively. "A great many wicked deeds have been committed by otherwise sane and rational men, haven't they? Things that they felt themselves justified in doing because they served some purpose."

"But whatever purpose can there be in killing innocent livestock?" Mrs. Millworth wondered.

At that moment, the gentlemen returned, looking slightly disheveled but also relieved.

"Has the magistrate arrived yet?" asked Mr. Millworth, rather out of breath as he pulled off his gloves.

"I daresay Mr. Marksham will take his own dear time in getting here, as has always been his habit," Mrs. Millworth replied, permitting herself a small snort of contempt, for she was not overly fond of the pompous and self-important gentleman. "In the meantime, do sit and tell us what you have discovered." The gentlemen strode into the drawing room where the ladies sat with their embroidery and took seats near the fire.

"There is no danger to the household," said Doctor Larkin reassuringly. "I apologize, most sincerely, for alarming you madam, but I had to be certain that no harm would come to any member of your home."

He glanced at Ellen's face as he spoke, and she imagined she saw a brief flash of some intense emotion in eyes before he looked back at Mrs. Millworth. Her heart gave a sudden leap in response, but she immediately ordered herself to ignore the feeling. It was simply nonsense to have such a reaction, as if a physician not wanting harm to befall a household was equated to a declaration of love. Truly, Ellen thought, her heart was decidedly untrustworthy.

She noticed Arabella looking at her curiously and put aside her mental scolding for the time being in order to better attend to what the gentlemen were saying.

"From what we can tell the flock was given a portion of grain that had been doused in a toxin," the doctor was explaining. "There was some remaining, scattered along the fence line of the pasture."

"Edwards is quite certain that no one here gave the flock any grain this past week. Indeed, he all but offered to swear to it on the Holy Bible, his mother's grave, and anything else we might wish," interjected Mr. Millworth helpfully.

"Edwards is the man with the sick little boy, isn't he? Doubtless he is worried that suspicions will be cast his way," Lord Willingham observed, and Ellen saw and interpreted the warm, tender look that crept into Arabella's eyes as he spoke. He might have been fully prepared to leap into action and strike down any evildoers, which was reassuring, but Ellen knew that her oldest friend would find the fact that he knew and considered the ailing child to be equally endearing.

"Why, we have already assured him repeatedly that no one would consider such a thing for an instant," Mrs. Millworth protested.

"I agree with you, of course," Doctor Larkin said, his voice steady and calming. "And I believe the evidence will clear his name from even a whisper of suspicion, but until such time, the man is understandably nervous. I have collected samples of the tainted grain and will analyze them further, but from simple observation alone I am certain they are the source of the poison. It would be extraordinarily difficult, if not outright impossible, for a man on such limited means as Edwards to procure such a quantity of laurel water."

"Laurel water? That is what killed all of those sheep?" Arabella asked, eyes widening.

"You are familiar with the substance?"

"Only to recognize the name, I am afraid. Marianne was reading of some incident involving the accidental misuse of it, and she happened to mention it to me. It's made from the leaves of cherry laurels, isn't it?"

"That is correct," Doctor Larkin agreed, nodding at Arabella as if she were a particularly clever student. Ellen felt the oddest flash of annoyance that *she* had not known the bit of trivia. After all, Marianne might just as easily have mentioned it to her as to Arabella, the girl seemed to bubble over with information at all hours, which was ludicrous, of course. What difference did it make that Arabella knew the item, and she did not?

"There aren't any cherry laurels growing anywhere around here. I asked Marianne when she spoke of it last year, and she assured me that there are none for miles as far as she knows," offered Arabella. "And you know Marianne, she would know, botany has been one of her pet interests for years and years now. She even hopes one day to take the crown of Northwick's best garden from Lady Mayberry."

"Unlikely," voiced Mrs. Millworth softly.

"True," Arabella agreed poking a needle into her work. "I told her the work is futile, but she does not listen to me."

"As it happens, I can confirm that no cherry laurels grow locally; not that I would risk making such a fool of myself as to doubt your sister's knowledge," said the doctor with a small chuckle. "If she turns her attention to medicine, I daresay she would surpass my own skill as a physician within a matter of months. But back to the matter at hand, I made a search for cherry laurels when I first came here and discovered that they do not grow well in this area at all. Laurel water *can* be used as a medicine, in small and careful amounts, and I had hoped to make something of a study on how the benefits of the substance might be retained while removing the risks."

"So," Mr. Millworth said thoughtfully. "Edwards could not possibly have distilled laurel water himself, even if he possessed the requisite knowledge and equipment, which is most unlikely. He certainly could not afford to purchase such a quantity."

"I think not," Dr. Larkin said.

"If Edwards had somehow come into such an amount of money, he would spend it on medicine and treatment for his child, not poison," put in Lord Willingham, with such an air of certainty that Ellen realized he must have spoken with the man extensively enough to have taken a measure of his character. She was quite certain he was correct, too, from everything she had seen in her own visits to the family's small cottage.

"These facts exonerate Edwards quite plainly, I am sure, and that needs to be made clear to everyone in the village," Mrs. Millworth declared. "Even a vague suspicion can be nearly as damaging to a man's reputation as an outright conviction of crime."

"I can attest to the veracity of *that*," agreed Lord Willingham with a rueful smile. Arabella briefly laid her hand upon his arm in silent reassurance, and Ellen found herself fighting against a sudden urge to cry. It was silly, she told herself, but the small evidence of their obvious affection and support for one another was so touching. She had wanted that very thing, love, so badly that she had been almost eager to be deceived by Sir James Randall.

PART II

CHAPTER 9

At that moment Mr. Marksham, the magistrate, was announced, and all attention turned to that gentleman as he entered the room. Almost comical in his air of bluster and self-importance, Marksham was a stout gentleman in his thirties. His balding head always seemed to gleam with such luster that Ellen and Arabella had privately decided that he must deliberately polish it. A fact which proved all the more distracting, as the domed pate in question was right at eye level, for Mr. Marksham had not been blessed with great height.

"Well, Millworth, what seems to be the matter this time?" Mr. Marksham demanded without preamble. "You seem to be getting into something of a habit of summoning me over to your home at the most extraordinarily inconvenient times. Surely Miss Millworth here has not suffered *another* narrow escape from the clutches of some villain?"

The room went so palpably silent and horrified at the magistrate's tactless speech that he really ought to have noticed. He seemed to see nothing amiss with his statement, however, and continued to gaze impudently and expectantly at Mr. Millworth.

Ellen wanted to sink into the floorboards if such a thing were possible. She picked up her needlework and busied herself with it although her eyes had immediately swum with tears and she could not see the stitches. Oh, why was she so sensitive?

She could tell that her parents were both too amazed at such a display of bad manners to reply. For her own part, she could feel blood rushing furiously to her face in a bewildering mix of anger and embarrassment. How horrid, to have her foolish mistake cast up in such a manner. Arabella gave an indignant murmur on her behalf, but her attention was quickly diverted to Lord Willingham, who looked quite perfectly capable of violence at that moment.

It was Doctor Larkin who broke the ringing silence, gazing down upon the magistrate with a look of chilly disdain.

"It was *I* who sent for you, Mr. Marksham, on a matter that has nothing to do with the Millworth family other than peripherally. Their flock of sheep, unfortunately, are the most recent victims in a rash of deaths that has been plaguing the livestock in this village. It most certainly has nothing whatsoever to do with Miss Millworth. It is only due to the urgency of this situation that I am willing to overlook your appalling lapse of manners, for the time being, at least."

"As if I cared in the slightest what a professional man thinks of my manners. I don't ask the butcher if he approves of my behavior either, if that's any consolation to you, Larkin," snorted Mr. Marksham dismissively before turning his attention back to Mr. Millworth. "Lost a few sheep, have you, Millworth? I can't say as that seems to merit summoning me out here as if I were some sort of pet genie. I am a busy man, I will remind you, with a great deal of important matters to occupy my attention."

"I believe I may safely say I was am no happier to send for you than you were to be summoned, sir," Mr. Millworth replied evenly, but Ellen could plainly sense her father's anger, controlled for the moment yet burning brightly all the same.

"Doubtful," sniffed the magistrate insultingly.

"Oh, I assure you. However, no matter how many important matters are vying for your time, you cannot have failed to notice the sudden outbreak of misfortune that has befallen so many landowners hereabouts of late. As magistrate, I should have thought that you would be far more concerned with such events than you appear."

"Farm beasts do die on occasion, you know, it is hardly unheard of. I can't imagine what you think *I* can do to prevent such things from happening, nor should I wish to in most cases. Why my own rooster died not just a fortnight past. I tossed him in a soup."

"*These* animals did not die naturally or by chance, Mr. Marksham. They have been poisoned," declared Mr. Millworth firmly. "Deliberately poisoned, I tell you."

Watching carefully, Ellen thought she saw the pompous magistrate grow a shade paler, or perhaps even master the urge to wince at Mr. Millworth's statement. It was only for a fleeting instant, and then the man blustered on, swelling with more importance and authority than ever.

"Nonsense. I never heard of such errant nonsense in all of my days. As if anyone in their right mind would go about poisoning livestock, especially with the spate of bad luck the town has had with influenza and flooding the last few years. I have no doubt that your man in charge of the flock, Edwards, isn't it? The man has no doubt been careless and lazy and is now trying to avoid blame by concocting this wild story or more likely he wants to steal the meat himself. He has a shifty sort of look about him, I have always said. I'm frankly surprised that you would entertain such a pack of lies. The man should be dismissed out of hand."

"Edwards has said no such thing, and as for shifty, why *that* is errant nonsense," Mrs. Millworth exclaimed indignantly, although she was generally not very outspoken in company. "Edwards has been with us a great many years and has always shown himself to be honest and hardworking and diligent in every task."

"It is Doctor Larkin here who discovered what had befallen our flock," said Mr. Millworth quickly, before Mr. Marksham could reply with whatever condescending remark he was clearly on the verge of aiming at Mrs.

Millworth. "I asked the doctor to examine the sheep, knowing well his reputation as a gifted man of science. A fact you yourself must recall, seeing as he brought you back from the brink of the grave when you had that nasty bout of influenza two winters ago."

Mr. Marksham had the grace to look momentarily abashed, as if he had indeed forgotten that he owed his life to the doctor, but the moment passed almost immediately.

"No one denies that Doctor Larkin is good at his work," he said in a belittling tone, clearly feeling himself superior to any man who engaged in such a sordid thing as work. "But as a man of science I have no doubt that he will admit a sheep is a far cry from a human being, and is therefore, quite out of his realm of expertise."

"There are more physiological similarities that you might suppose, more in some cases than others, I should venture to say," Doctor Larkin said drily. "However, the question here is not of physiology, Mr. Marksham, but of poison. I assure that laurel water will kill a sheep quite as easily as it will kill a human being, and that is just what *did* kill Mr. Millworth's sheep."

"Nonsense," declared the magistrate again with great certainty.

"Indeed, it is not. I have not only positively identified the cause of death, but we have also found the contaminated grain that was given to the flock. There is no question at all in my mind. The evidence is overwhelmingly conclusive. We must find the culprit before he does more mischief."

"Ah, but that is just in your mind, as you say," replied Mr. Marksham with a half-hearted smile. "You might mutter Latin and Greek phrases, and fiddle with your medical equipment all day and *seem* very knowledgeable and certain, but no one else would have any idea what you were going on about, now would they? Who in these parts would be able to contradict your claims, no matter how preposterous? I daresay you've had a bit too much time on your hands of late, Doctor Larkin. You know we got along just fine with only old Doctor Harding in the town. We're a healthy sort in this village, barring an epidemic of influenza, of course, but there is really no need for you to go about trying to create excitement where there is none, you know, just so you can show off your education. I am sure we are all quite impressed with your intelligence already so I would advise you to stop needlessly upsetting people and wasting my time. Good evening to you all." He gave a curt nod of his head, put on his hat and turned towards the door.

The company stared after him in shock. Ellen could not believe that the man would not even deign to look at the evidence. It was preposterous.

CHAPTER 10

The magistrate took himself away, self-important indignation fairly oozing from every pore, and no one made any move to detain him. It was Ellen who broke the stunned silence, although she had not actually intended to speak aloud.

"What a horrible, odious, *useless* man." she exclaimed. She had forgotten his insult to her, it had faded to insignificance in the light of his despicable rudeness to Doctor Larkin.

"Oh, Ellen, not so loud," her mother remonstrated half-heartedly, a smile tugging at her lips despite her words. "He might still be able to hear you, you know how sound travels from this particular room."

"What can he do about it if he *does* overhear, bore her to death?" asked Lord Willingham, giving Ellen a friendly grin that clearly conveyed his approval of her sentiment.

"Well, he did go to school with the Duke of Bramblewood. I would think he could make trouble for you if he wished," added Mr. Millworth.

"*Pish Posh*," added Ellen. "The man is a peacock...and a ponce."

Her mother chuckled at the unintended alliteration.

"I won't claim those are the *precise* words I would have chosen to describe that idiot," Lord Willingham added, "but then, Miss Millworth is naturally much more refined than I could ever claim to be. It is funny, though, that I don't recall the magistrate being half such a fool the last time I saw him."

"The truth is, the last time you saw the man, you were handing him a wanted criminal already discovered and incapacitated," Mr. Millworth pointed out rather ruefully. "There was hardly any action required of him as magistrate other than to take a great deal of unearned credit and congratulate himself endlessly. In this case, we are only presenting him with a troublesome problem that has no obvious solution and will most likely take a good deal of effort to untangle."

"That's no excuse for the man to be so shockingly discourteous," averred Arabella. "I cannot claim to have ever thought very highly of him, but it was almost as if he came here determined to be as offensive as possible, especially to you, Doctor Larkin. It was very odd, I thought."

"It *is* hard to believe he would speak in such a manner to someone who had previously saved his life," agreed Lord Willingham.

"May I suggest that the next time he falls ill you refer him to his butcher?" Mr. Millworth said as he stood and went to the side table to fetch a decanter or brandy.

"That is certainly a tempting thought," Doctor Larkin said with a laugh and a slight shrug. "I have no doubt he will sing a different tune entirely once his gout flares up, as I predict it will before too much time passes judging by his complexion. But even when Mr. Marksham is in dire need of my care, he manages to make sure that I am aware of the fact that he is my superior, as a *true* gentleman does not have a profession."

"As if your family does not surpass his in rank, importance, and wealth, to say nothing of good taste and manners , a hundred times over," Mrs. Millworth declared heatedly.

Mr. Millworth held up the decanter of brandy with a question in his eyes. "Since we cannot currently have tea," he said. "I think we could all use something to calm our nerves." He turned to his wife. "Will you have a spate of sherry, my dear?" he asked.

After the ladies had been served sherry and the gentlemen, brandy, Doctor Larkin said. "I usually do not imbibe while working." Nonetheless, he took the glass. He seemed no less shaken than the others. "I must have my wits about me, lest that man call me a half-wit."

"He would not dare," interrupted Ellen and then she sipped the sherry, embarrassed at her own outburst.

"And what might be more noble than choosing to save lives, at the expense of your own health, I would wager, when you might be living a life of ease?" added her mother.

"I suspect you are my mother's anonymous well of information, madam," the doctor replied, bowing gallantly to Mrs. Millworth. "I know she has some hidden source in these parts who reports to her occasionally that I look as if I am not taking proper care of myself."

"And no more do you," she answered unrepentantly, giving him a fond smile. "If you want me to write more encouraging observations in my next correspondence with Lady Larkin, then you might consider eating a proper meal or two, perhaps even resting for an entire day."

"I will heed your advice at the earliest possible time, and do not imagine that I mind for a moment what Mr. Marksham thinks of me personally. My concern is that he has dismissed the matter so thoroughly, and we have no reason to think that these deaths today will be the last."

"Well, that is no great matter. I imagine we can investigate rather more effectively without the magistrate's assistance than with it," Lord Willingham stated briskly, looking decidedly enthusiastic at the idea.

"*That* is certainly true enough," Mr. Millworth remarked drily. "Although I would not put it past Marksham to block us wherever he can out of sheer obstinance. He is not, I dare say you have already gathered, the sort of man who takes kindly to being contradicted. The very thought of being proven wrong may very well make him double down and refuse to concede that he was in error, even if we were to catch the villain red-handed in the market square."

"There isn't much he can do to stop us from speaking with the other landowners who have experienced this tragedy, though," pointed out Arabella. "And I should think that they would be rather eager to discover a reason for their misfortunes."

"If you were able to examine the bodies of the livestock that had been stricken earlier, would you still be able to detect any evidence of poison?" wondered Lord Willingham. "Or is that a foolish question, Larkin? I readily confess myself to be most thoroughly ignorant of all such matters."

"It is not a foolish question at all. I believe in this case, there might be a way to detect some lingering traces on the more recent corpses, if there has not been too much decay. More importantly, to my mind, we must speak to those landowners to obtain permission to search for any remaining poisoned grain that may be scattered about. For one thing it would be clear evidence, and for another it is hardly advisable to leave even a handful of such a thing where any unfortunate creature might come across it."

"I had not considered that," said Mrs. Millworth with a slight shudder. "And the animals that died, I suppose they are not safe to consume?"

"Decidedly not," agreed the doctor firmly. "Which is another reason that the magistrate's refusal to even entertain the idea that these animals have been poisoned is so dangerous. So far everyone seems to have had the sense to just dispose of the dead livestock, erring on the side of caution. I have not treated anyone for any symptoms of poisoning, at least. But there *are* hungry families hereabouts, and desperation can cancel out sense in even the most rational of men. We must not endanger any lives by keeping this matter quiet."

"But if we *say* that all of these animals have been poisoned, won't Mr. Marksham feel the need to accuse someone, just to hurry the matter along?" Ellen asked hesitantly. "He seemed to have a scapegoat picked out already, accusing poor Edwards of carelessness and calling him shifty the way he did. He would have the authority to arrest Edwards, wouldn't he?"

Lord Willingham nodded. "He would."

The faces of the assembled group all shifted to consternation at that idea, so rapidly and uniformly as to be almost comical, had the situation not been so serious. Ellen watched Arabella's brow furrow with concentration for a moment, and then clear swiftly as a triumphant light gleamed in her eyes.

"What have you thought of, Arabella?" Lord Willingham asked, clearly also having observed the progressive changes in her expression.

"Ellen is undoubtedly correct. I think that accusing Edwards is just what that horrid man would do once there was some sort of public outcry at the idea of livestock being poisoned. *But*, as you have said, Mr. Millworth, Mr. Marksham is not the sort of man who will easily admit to being wrong. I think all we must do to protect Edwards is to maneuver Mr. Marksham into publicly declaring his opinion that the animals have *not* been poisoned. He cannot very well arrest a man for poisoning livestock while also insisting that they haven't been poisoned, after all."

"Such a clever and devious mind you have," observed Lord Willingham with an equal measure of admiration and humor. "It is fortunate indeed for your future husband that he is utterly and eternally devoted to you, else you would undoubtedly make him suffer." He grinned at her belying his words.

"Endlessly, and you do well to realize it, sir," returned Arabella with a merry laugh that was so infectious as to break apart a good deal of the tension in the room.

"I believe you are entirely right, on both matters, as it were," Mrs. Millworth declared, sending Arabella a dimpling smile. "And it will be practically child's play to coax a public declaration from Mr. Marksham. I daresay we can accomplish that before tomorrow afternoon, not that you gentlemen really need wait on that to begin speaking in confidence to the other landowners."

The small party broke up then, with considerably lighter spirits than when they had first assembled, thanks to a plan of action and a sense of purpose.

CHAPTER 11

After a leisurely breakfast the next morning, Ellen accompanied her mother into the village to meet Arabella so that they might put their scheme into action. She supposed it *would* be a simple enough matter to goad the ridiculous magistrate into blustering publicly that Doctor Larkin's idea of poison was all nonsense. Particularly with Arabella Sedgewick leading the charge, she thought with a small smile.

Years of practice keeping the peace in the Sedgewick family had certainly honed Arabella's skill at maneuvering people, and generally without their notice. Ellen had always been amazed at Arabella's ability to set aside her own feelings whenever the occasion called for it. She would certainly be able to smile sweetly into Mr. Marksham's ruddy face while leading him to say exactly what she wished. Ellen would consider herself lucky if she managed to look demure and pleasant during the planned interlude, for surely her manner would give away how much she loathed the man.

"What are you thinking, my darling?" wondered Mrs. Millworth when a little sigh escaped Ellen's lips.

"Oh, I was thinking of how infuriating Mr. Marksham is, and wishing that I had half of Arabella's skill at concealing her private feelings," Ellen confessed ruefully. "I really do envy her. I have never come close to mastering that particular art. All of *my* emotions are revealed on my face straightaway, no matter how I try to school my expression."

"And I daresay Arabella envies your candor, dearest child. We are all always wishing for the attributes in which we feel deficient, while overlooking one's own strengths altogether. It is the way of the world, after all. But fortunately, Mr. Marksham is not a man to entertain the notion that anyone might be anything short of awed by his marvelousness. He is not likely to notice if you *do* look disgusted with him."

"Thank providence for that," replied Ellen with a smile at her mother's bluntly stated assessment of the magistrate. "Although it is also likely the very reason that I find him so odious. His rudeness to Doctor Larkin last evening was nothing short of unforgiveable, and I can scarcely bear the idea that shortly we will be providing him with an opportunity to repeat his slanderous implications publicly."

"There isn't a soul in the village who will value Mr. Marksham's blathering over Roger Larkin's good sense," Mrs. Millworth stated firmly, a decisive ring in her voice even as she narrowed her pretty eyes speculatively at her daughter. "The doctor's reputation speaks for itself, and I am sure everyone values him a great deal more than that. It is a mystery to *me* how the gentleman has managed to remain unmarried for so long, even as a younger son. He is so handsome and has a generous spirit, to say nothing of his talent as a physician. I imagine all the young ladies are simply wild for him."

"Mmm," Ellen murmured, averting her gaze and ordering herself not to blush. Of course, it did not matter to her if *dozens* of young ladies were chasing after the doctor. She cast about hastily for a way to redirect the conversation. "Perhaps you are right, Mama. Indeed, I hope you are. Only a great fool would take Mr. Marksham's word over Doctor Larkin's. Really, I cannot imagine how he ever was named magistrate except that he went to school with the Duke of Brambleton."

"It is nepotism, plain and simple," Mrs. Millworth said, "giving such positions to those of acquaintance instead of those with the most talent to do the job well. Unfortunately, that is the way of the world," Arabella said.

"Oh my," Ellen sighed.

"What is it?" her mother asked.

"It is just I do not look forward to this charade. I am silly to work myself up over a conversation that has not even happened yet," Ellen added. "Particularly when we do not even know for certain if we will have an opportunity to speak with the horrid man today."

"Oh, he flattered the right people, which can be said for a great many of those in office," answered Mrs. Millworth with one last shrewd glance at her daughter's downcast eyes. "Although fortunately, most of them do not even approach the pinnacle of incompetence which Mr. Marksham has achieved. But as for not speaking with him this morning, I think you may safely assume that we will. Whatever he may claim about having a great many important matters vying for his attention, scarcely a day goes by that he does not spend several hours strutting from one shop to another so that as many people as possible may be granted the opportunity to be impressed."

"Now that you mention it, I can hardly think of a time that I visited the shops in the village and Mr. Marksham was *not* somewhere about," said Ellen.

The pair walked on in companionable silence for a short time until they were overtaken by not only Arabella, but both of her younger sisters as well. Marianne Sedgewick's eyes were alight with what Ellen knew was sheer delight at the prospect of a puzzle that needed to be solved, while Daphne seemed caught between her customary mischievous excitement and her newfound resolve to comport herself in a more ladylike manner.

"You can see I have brought my entire family into our little venture," said Arabella rather apologetically once they had all exchanged affectionate greetings. "I felt it best to inform Father of Doctor Larkin's discovery. He fully credits Doctor Larkin's opinion, by the way, and decided to accompany Mr. Millworth and the doctor this morning in their calls. But then, naturally, nothing else would do, but for Marianne and Daphne to come along with us."

"We insisted quite shamelessly," Marianne agreed, smiling, as she fell into stride with the others.

"And quite right, too," said Mrs. Millworth fondly, her affection for all the Sedgewick girls plainly evident. "Actually, I think this will be to our benefit. Daphne, dear, do you think that when we encounter Mr. Marksham you might be equal to the task of bringing up the matter of the poison that Doctor Larkin detected? Rather impulsively, you know, and not at a terribly discrete volume."

"Oh, yes, that would do very well," said Arabella at once, catching on to Mrs. Millworth's idea. "And it would seem perfectly natural. Not that you haven't made great strides in becoming more refined and decorous, Daphne," she added with a loving smile for her youngest sister.

"I don't believe I shall mind putting my progress aside briefly, since it is for a good cause," laughed Daphne merrily. The youngest Sedgewick sister was extraordinarily pretty, and one of the best-hearted people that Ellen knew, but she had an impulsive and rather heedless nature that had been allowed perhaps more free rein than was advisable until fairly recently.

"Look, there is Mr. Marksham coming out of the haberdasher's just now. That shiny pate of his is like a beacon even from all the way across the town square," observed Ellen, making everyone laugh as they entered the bustling main thoroughfare of the village.

"And he seems to be going to the jeweler's shop, which is quite providential," said Arabella, a steely glint of determination in her eyes. "I actually do need to stop there, for Mr. Tremont sent word to me yesterday that the necklace I had asked him to repair is ready. Daphne, you must wait for us to assure ourselves that there are plenty of other people close enough at hand to overhear our conversation."

The ladies made their way into the jewelry maker's shop, a place that had always seemed wonderfully fascinating and magical to Ellen in her childhood. Crossing the threshold, all of her attention was fixed upon keeping her expression serene as she looked about the shop hoping to see one or two of the more notorious gossips of the village. She was unprepared to be struck by a vivid memory of the last time she had been in the establishment, a mere handful of days before the scoundrel's attempted abduction of her.

Sir Randall had insisted on commissioning several rather elaborate pieces of jewelry, which were to have been wedding presents for his bride, and had wanted her to come with him in order to consult her taste. It had all felt thrillingly romantic at the time, his bold declarations to Mr. Tremont that no expense was to be spared and that he would consider only the finest jewels as fit adornment for his beloved Ellen. Those speeches, she realized, had been as ostentatious as the commissioned jewelry itself, and had certainly been for the benefit of everyone listening.

He had lavishly claimed that her beauty outshone every gem in the shop, nay, in the world. But he had not murmured those observations softly, intimately into her ear as he would have done earlier in their connection. Her affection had already been won, her blind and trusting loyalty was unquestioningly his by that time. The purpose of the entire foray that day, Ellen saw, with utter clarity and certainty, had been to ensure that everyone else in the village believed his claims of undying love. People had begun to wonder if he were only interested in her fortune, so he had countered those suspicions with a show of great love and wealth.

"Dearest, you look so pale suddenly," Mrs. Millworth's voice mercifully cut through Ellen's thoughts. She laid a loving hand on her daughter's arm. "I had thought the walk was doing you some good, but perhaps you have over done it. Are you tired?"

"No, I am quite well, Mama," Ellen said, lifting her chin slightly in determination. The memory of Sir Randall would not be allowed to keep her out of a place she had always loved. "I was just hoping that dear Mr. Tremont was not terribly burdened by all the pieces that were commissioned on my behalf a few months ago."

"You need not worry about that, your father met with Mr. Tremont almost at once and fortunately only one piece had been begun. Mr. Tremont assured him that he would experience no difficulties in that regard," her mother answered at a discrete volume.

Ellen nodded her approval of the matter and tried to put the treacherous thoughts behind her.

CHAPTER 12

The jewelry maker's shop was not as well-populated as the group of ladies would have wished, and Arabella gave Daphne a slight shake of the head to signal that she should not approach Mr. Marksham. The magistrate had evidently cornered the jeweler's assistant in a detailed discussion comparing the merits of one ornate buckle to another, and took no notice of anyone else.

"Ah, good morning to you, ladies," Mr. Tremont said in a low voice. He had slipped behind his counter at the jingle of the shop door with a rather wary expression on his face which cleared when he caught sight of the party. A small, almost frail man with watery blue eyes blinking behind owlish spectacles, Mr. Tremont habitually spoke in a low voice. But it was obvious to Ellen that on this particular occasion he was hoping to avoid the notice of Mr. Marksham. Understanding, the women exchanged pleasantries with the jeweler in equally soft tones.

"I was quite surprised to receive your note yesterday, Mr. Tremont," said Arabella. "I had no idea that you would be able to complete the repair so rapidly, but I am delighted, of course."

"A clasp is a simple enough thing to mend, Lady Sedgewick, and I started on it almost the moment that you left the necklace here. It was my own creation, you know. The earl had it made for your mother all those many years ago. I greatly dislike seeing my work fail."

"You certainly must not blame yourself," Arabella said with a reassuring smile. "It was through no fault of yours that the clasp came to be broken."

"Indeed, it would have needed to be made of iron to withstand the treatment that it received," put in Marianne with an arch look at Daphne.

"It's entirely my fault," the girl agreed readily. "But in my defense, I *was* only six or seven-years-old at the time. I had been playing in our mother's jewel case, even though I knew it was not allowed, and could not get the clasp undone. When I heard footsteps coming up the passageway, I wrenched the necklace off in a panic."

"It was horribly naughty of you, but we never minded that so much. It was unfortunate that you chose *that* occasion to be one of the few times that you ever bothered to avoid your naughtiness being detected," Arabella said with fond exasperation. "I was quite dismayed to discover the damage, years later."

"I hope you will not think too poorly of me for being relieved to hear the tale," Mr. Tremont chuckled gently.

"Particularly as it explains the traces of what I believe to have once been jam. All cleared away now, of course. If you will allow me to fetch the necklace from my workbench, I shall only be a moment."

The slight, refined man retreated to the back room of the shop, reappearing almost immediately with a small velvet case. Opening it with a little flourish, he revealed a delicate necklace of exquisite pearls, gleaming enticingly.

"Oh, the times I saw your mother wearing this necklace," Mrs. Millworth murmured, her voice heavy with sentiment. "It was her favorite adornment, I think. It certainly brings back a host of lovely memories."

"I mean to wear it on my wedding day," said Arabella softly, unshed tears glimmering in her eyes. "I thought it would be like having her with me, in a way."

"Of course it will be, dear," said Mrs. Millworth, placing a gentle hand on Arabella's shoulder in comfort. Ellen was profoundly grateful that her mother had always been so willing to stand in for the late Lady Sedgewick, easing at least a little of the pain that the Sedgewick sisters lived with being devoid of a mother's love. It seemed so unfair that Arabella's joy on her wedding day would be tinged with that sorrow. Sir Randall's greatest mistake had been in thinking that she would have willingly eloped with him and been married without her family present. She had been in his thrall, but not so entirely as *that* and the idea that he would think her family unimportant told just how little he knew his future bride's sensibilities.

At that moment the door to the jewelry maker's shop swung open with another cheerful tinkle, and in swept an extensive bevy of women, several of whom Ellen recognized with satisfaction as some of the most avid gossips in the village. She grinned at Arabella with undisguised glee.

Arabella smiled at Ellen and then turned, holding up a discrete finger to Daphne for a moment, signaling to the young girl that she ought to wait a few moments more. Impatience seemed to roll off of Daphne in tangible waves, but she remained quiet while Arabella continued to calmly talk with Mr. Tremont about an engraved case that she wanted him to create as a wedding gift for Lord Willingham.

When Mrs. Millworth gave Daphne a subtle nod, Ellen half expected the girl to race for Mr. Marksham like a hound after a fox, but to her credit she merely began to stroll in a leisurely manner to a display of pretty trinkets near the center of the shop. Picking through the baubles carelessly, she was perfectly positioned to be in the magistrate's line of sight when he finally released the harried assistant, having evidently decided that neither buckle was quite up to his high standards.

"Oh. Mr. Marksham," exclaimed Daphne, giving a remarkably natural start when the man turned in her direction and unintentionally made eye contact. "How marvelous to run into you. Metaphorically speaking, of course, not like the last time we saw one another. I'm still awfully sorry about your waistcoat, I hope you will believe I never *intended* to splash so much tea all over you. Indeed, I never intended to splash any. It was a very full teacup, and terribly hot, too, I fear."

"Er, yes, that is to say…" began the magistrate in some confusion, but Daphne chattered brightly and ruthlessly over him, drawing the amused attention of everyone in the shop to her words.

"I ought to have said 'how marvelous to *see* you' I suppose, and not have been so tactless as to remind you of that unpleasant incident, but I didn't think of it until after I had already spoken. That happens to me a great deal, you know, it is most vexing. Although, of course speaking tactlessly is not half so bad as accidentally scalding someone with tea, even if he *did* decide to stand terribly close by without announcing himself. Not that it's your fault, sir, for I ought not to have been gesturing so expansively and forgotten that I was holding a cup of tea."

"Quite so…" Mr. Marksham attempted once more to interrupt Daphne with no better success.

"*Did* it scald your skin half off?" Daphne asked, her voice raising in volume. "Arabella said that it must have, and she was very cross with me. I hope that was only an exaggeration on her part, to make me see the error of my ways and the importance of cultivating better manners. If she wasn't exaggerating, I hope you had Doctor Larkin to attend to your injury. Not that you could have had anyone else, as he *is* a perfectly lovely doctor don't you think? And so clever. Why, did you know, he discovered that all the sheep and cattle and things that have been dying lately were *poisoned*?" Her voice rose in indignation at the thought. "Had you heard that, Mr. Marksham? Of course, you must have, how silly of me," Daphne continued unabated. "Naturally a gentleman with an important position such a magistrate would hear about something like that long before a little girl would. *You* were probably told directly, too, and not reduced to clandestinely listening to your older sisters' conversation as I was. Nevertheless, it is shocking news, isn't it? Poison? Someone going about in the dead of night, I imagine it would have to be done in the dead of night in order to avoid detection, don't you think?"

"Well, I..." began the magistrate, but Daphne kept right on speaking.

"Committing such foul deeds. I do hope you catch whoever it is quite soon, and not only for the sake of the poor livestock, I must confess. I am so wildly curious about who would do such a thing, and *why*, I declare I shall not have a moment's peace until I know. That is why I was excited to run into..." She paused as if just realizing how she was running on. Daphne seemed to regain her composure. "I mean, to see you just now. I have been wishing to speak with you and there you appear, just as if I had summoned you like a genie. I wanted particularly to ask if you think you shall find the criminal soon?"

Daphne paused, ostensibly to take a breath, although Ellen knew from direct experience that the child was perfectly capable of prattling on incessantly for a great deal longer. Nearly everyone present had gasped in dismay when she uttered the word *poison*, and expressions had gone rapidly from amusement to varying degrees of shock and distress.

Having neatly laid her trap for Mr. Marksham, Daphne gazed at the man in expectant silence, her eyes wide, an air of unstudied innocence gracing her every feature. Mr. Marksham, Ellen was pleased to see, was turning an ever-deeper shade of red with suppressed anger. He would not dare to scold the Earl's youngest child, although he clearly yearned to do so, for no matter how much he might puff himself up he was still aware of Lord Sedgewick's importance and influence. "It is just so awful. Do you not think so? I do pray that you will find the culprit soon," Daphne said. "You will, won't you?"

Ellen held her breath hoping Mr. Marksham would not accuse the hapless Edwards there and then, but he did not.

CHAPTER 13

With all eyes upon him and the silence in the shop ringing all the more palpably in the sudden absence of Daphne's bubbling chatter, the magistrate had no choice but to answer her question.

"Ah, pray do not be needlessly alarmed, my dear child," he said, his customary condescension sounding a trifle strained. "I have no doubt that it is unhealthy for delicate young ladies to become excited over such a trivial matter as a few unfortunate animals. They would have been slaughtered for dinner, had they not taken ill, so they would have died soon enough as it were."

"Oh, but they weren't just taken ill, were they?" asked Daphne persistently. "They were deliberately killed, and not so that they could be eaten. Indeed, I heard my sister saying that the doctor was quite certain that anyone who ate them would be poisoned in turn too. Isn't that awful? Poisoned." Daphne's voice rose on the last word so that no one in the shop could have failed to hear her horrified wail.

"Good Heavens, Mr. Marksham, this is dreadful." exclaimed Lady Evans, thrusting her reticule into her niece's patient arms and breaking into the conversation without ceremony. "Something must be done at once, before someone is killed. What do you plan to do?"

Being interrogated by Lady Evans, who was the magistrate's closest neighbor and bitterest foe, seemed to be more than Mr. Marksham's composure could endure. He swelled visibly with indignation, putting a mighty strain on his waistcoat buttons, and turned several shades darker red, so that he resembled nothing so much as a large beet, Ellen thought irreverently.

"Now, now, I can assure you that there is no danger, madam," he declared hotly. "Let us not make a panic simply on the word of a, shall I say, impressionable young girl who may have misinterpreted what she overheard her elders discussing. It would be the height of folly to create an uproar, I say."

"I did not misinterpret." Daphne interjected haughtily.

"I am not suggesting that we *do* make a panic on the word of a young girl. Although I daresay I have never met anyone less likely to be described with the word 'impressionable' than Miss Daphne." retorted Lady Evans crisply. "But leaving that aside for the moment, it is the word of Doctor Larkin that concerns me."

"Quite so," agreed another woman encouragingly.

"Why, if Roger Larkin says that those beasts were poisoned, then you may take it is a fact that they were. I was saying only the other day, don't you recall my saying, Mary, that Doctor Larkin is a perfectly brilliant man?"

"Yes, you said just that, Aunt Agatha," agreed the long-suffering Miss Stanton in colorless tones.

"I've said it a dozen times if I've said it once. It's quite true," interjected Mrs. Potterton, evidently not wanting to be outdone. "But my question is, Mr. Marksham, *does* Doctor Larkin say that all the dead livestock have been poisoned?"

Although Daphne had been easing out of the center of the shop, content to let the older women take over from there, she drew up sharply at that question.

"Of course, he does, I wouldn't invent something like —" she began indignantly, but Marianne hastily drew her back.

"Well?" demanded Lady Evans, pinning Mr. Marksham with a formidable glare.

"And what if he does?" the man blustered. "He might say anything he likes. He does say anything he likes, for all any of us know. But I tell you those animals were not poisoned. The very notion is absurd. I did not rise to my position by gullibly believing every nonsensical opinion that is presented to me. I have examined the matter and there is nothing to convince *me* that those creatures died by any reason other than illness or perhaps neglect. What possible reason could anyone have to do such a thing?"

"But what possible reason could the doctor have for making such a serious claim?" asked Lady Gatwick in a reasonable tone, evidently seeing that her companions were too distraught to speak calmly.

"I would not care to speculate on that," answered the magistrate with great dignity, smoothing his waistcoat and seeming to feel that he had finally gained the upper hand. "As it is difficult to ascribe any charitable motivation to the lad's claim, and I hold myself to a standard that does not permit evil-minded gossip. However, since you insist upon knowing my thoughts on the matter, I will say that it seems clear enough to me. Either Larkin has made a simple error in his diagnosis, which I may say frankly seems perfectly likely to me, such things being remarkably difficult, or he has some private reason for wanting to cause an uproar in our community. It may be that he wants to impress some young lady, or perhaps he is finding our quiet, peaceful village a trifle dull for his taste. He may even be a trifle unbalanced; I believe I read somewhere that such a thing is quite common among the sort of men who dabble in medical science. But whatever his reason is, the fact remains, I am sure, that those animals died of perfectly naturally causes."

"You thought that 'lad' as you call him seemed balanced enough when he saved your life last winter," Lady Evans pointed out, battle light shining plainly in her face. But Mr. Marksham had had enough.

"That is hardly relevant, madam. I was appointed the magistrate of this community, and as such I have given this issue, my thorough consideration and deemed that the livestock have most decidedly *not* been poisoned. That is my final word, and you must all trust my judgement. Now, I hope that I have fully explained my view on the matter, for I have far too many matters of *actual* importance to attend to and I cannot be expected to waste any more of my time on a pack of wild conjecture."

Bowing slightly to the shop at large, Mr. Marksham made a far hastier exit than his bulk would ordinarily have allowed. An excited murmuring began to rise up in his wake, as the various women began to discuss and speculate. Some looked rather thrilled at the prospect of having a new and fascinating topic of discussion, others looked genuinely alarmed and distressed, and still others were indignant over the magistrate's rude speech.

Ellen was pleased to see that no one seemed to have any doubt that what Doctor Larkin said was true, and more than a few women were fairly outraged at the disrespectful aspersions that Mr. Marksham had laid upon the doctor's character.

"I never heard such nonsense. He was appointed magistrate, more's the pity, but that hardly makes Mr. Marksham entitled to unquestioning obedience, which is what he seems to want from everyone in the village," said one matron indignantly, close at hand to Ellen. "And as for more pressing matters requiring his attention, why I should dearly love to know what might be more urgent than this. People's livelihoods and perhaps even their very lives are at risk until this is resolved, what could be more important than that?"

"Well, he *did* have to spend a quarter of an hour here, examining buckles and things. It seemed to be a matter of life or death, particularly when nothing here was quite ostentatious enough," said Ellen mischievously, making the woman blink in surprise for a moment before bursting into laughter.

"Oh, certainly. I cannot imagine what I was thinking," she said dryly. "I had forgotten for a moment the great importance of finding just the right buckle, how silly of me."

"I have known Mr. Marksham since we were both children, and he is a greater fool now than he was fifty years ago," Lady Evans was announcing stridently to everyone in the shop. "And I may say that *that* is saying something."

The conversations turned from abusing the magistrate to proposing various candidates for the role of poisoner, and Ellen slipped out of the shop along with her mother and friends and a number of other ladies who were evidently eager to spread the titillating news far and wide.

"Well, that was certainly a rousing success," Arabella stated once they had reached the relative privacy of the outskirts of the village. "I will be very surprised indeed if Doctor Larkin has anyone left to warn within an hour's time."

"You were simply perfect, Daphne, babbling on like a little brook and yet leading Mr. Marksham precisely where you wanted. *I* will be very surprised if he is not still puzzling over half of the things you said next week." laughed Ellen, giving Daphne an impulsive embrace.

The girl smiled winsomely up at her, and Ellen realized she felt more content than she had in months. She and Daphne had always been similar in some ways, carefree and talkative, two traits which Ellen had feared she had lost forever. Perhaps it was her refusal to be overwhelmed by the unbidden memories of Sir Randall that had greeted her at the jewel maker's door, which seemed to be a very trivial matter in the light of everything else, but she somehow felt that she had rounded an invisible, secret corner when she had triumphed in that small battle.

It had been almost startling, realizing that she was comfortably speaking and even making jests with the very people that she had avoided so assiduously ever since her abduction. Their attention was riveted to a new scandal, which helped, of course, but Ellen suspected that even when the current outrage died away, she would still feel more confident inserting herself into conversations. It was immensely satisfying to contemplate.

"My ability to babble like a brook shouldn't be such a great surprise," Daphne returned merrily. "I should think you all would be instead congratulating me on my self-restraint. I don't believe I have ever wanted to kick anyone in the shins quite so heartily as I did just then when he called me an impressionable little girl."

"It *was* insufferable of him," agreed Marianne. "And you were a perfect angel of composure. You shall just have to quench your righteous wrath with the knowledge that you caused him quite a great deal of distress."

"And if that knowledge is not quite sufficient, you always have the memory of scalding the wretched man with hot tea not so very long ago," added Mrs. Millworth helpfully, causing the entire party to burst out spontaneously with long-suppressed laughter.

CHAPTER 14

Ellen walked briskly along the narrow path that led to the simple cottage where the Edwards family dwelt. She was laden with a rather heavy basket, but there was a certain satisfaction in carrying the burden herself, in venturing out of her home alone, and in refusing to remain on the periphery of life any longer.

It had been rather difficult for her to hold on to the sense of victory at outwitting the magistrate over the course of the following days, despite her greatly improved health and spirits, but she was determined to pursue the sensation doggedly.

She ordered herself to remember all the hopeful things that had occurred since the morning in Mr. Tremont's shop. Mr. Millworth had reported that the gentlemen had encountered no difficulty in persuading the other landowners to listen to the doctor's explanation, and their luck had even gone so far as to enable them to discover traces of poisoned grain on two additional fields.

The consensus was that although the reason anyone might have for doing such a thing was shrouded in mystery, it was clear enough that Doctor Larkin' pronouncement was to be listened to no matter how forcefully the magistrate might decry it. It was reasonable to assume that no one, no matter how destitute, would risk death by consuming the dead livestock, which was a comfort. Distressingly, though, there were more stricken animals than ever.

Lord Willingham, along with Mr. Millworth, the Earl, and other owners of large estates in the area, had all taken the precaution of assigning men to guard their herds constantly. This had been largely successful, and Ellen knew that Lord Willingham was especially anxious about the safety of his horses, going so far as to take up sentry duty himself several nights, as Arabella had told her. The downside seemed to be that the perpetrator had been discouraged by the additional security from striking at the larger estates as previously, and had taken to poisoning the livestock of much smaller farms. Many of those could ill afford the loss of even a single animal, making the losses altogether devastating.

They might have been successful in keeping suspicions from being cast on Edwards, but even greater than their attempts was the fact that Edwards himself had lost the sole cow he owned. A creature whose milk was vitally important for the recovery of his frail little son. Ellen knew that the family had saved and sacrificed greatly to purchase the animal, and it seemed bitterly unfair that they should have lost it in such a senseless manner.

She had heard of the misfortune the day before, but heavy rains had prevented her from making her long-overdue visit then. Indeed, the path was still terribly muddy, making her progress difficult enough that she knew her parents would have insisted she send the basket with someone else. It might have been a more sensible option, but Ellen hardly cared. She was quite finished with being passive and letting others shoulder her burdens. Besides, she had been feeling guilty for not visiting the cottage in so long when she had formerly gone at least twice a week.

To her surprise, Ellen heard laughter ringing out from the open door of the little cottage as she approached. She had expected to find the family in a somber state of mind, knowing how Mrs. Edwards had pinned her hope for her child's recovery on the friendly little Guernsey cow Edwards had been so proud to purchase.

Just as she came up to the shallow stone step, Doctor Larkin appeared in the doorway, a smile blooming on his face endearingly.

"Miss Millworth." he exclaimed at the sight of her. "Good Heavens, did you walk here in all this mud?"

"Yes," she answered shortly, knowing that she was being rude, feeling a stubborn frown threatening to tug at her expression. If only he would stop treating her like a fragile patient, and notice that she was a woman, but a patient, she reminded herself, was exactly what she was, and she had no business wishing to be anything else to the doctor, and yet she had no inclination of how to make him notice her as a woman, rather than a patient.

"Well, the activity certainly agrees with you," he said with professional curtesy. "I cannot think of a time that you ever looked…" he faltered a moment and then said, "in better health."

"I feel quite healthy," she said. "No doubt the crisp air has done me good, but I'm sure my color is high and my cheeks are unfashionably red with the cold."

"I think you look lovely," He breathed, and then he quickly amended, "If you will forgive my impertinence in saying so."

She stared at him for a long moment. It was an absurd thing for him to say, when her petticoats were all spattered with mud and her hair was most certainly in a state of wild disarray from the combination of wind and exertion. But she could not help being pleased by the absurdity, nevertheless, and she looked at him quite steadily, wondering if he had for just a moment noticed that she was a woman instead of just his patient. Could it be so?

"Oh, you are far too kind," she laughed, not even caring that a blush was surely spreading across her cheeks to cause them to be more crimson than the cold had warranted. "I must apologize for my rudeness just now, I fear. I was certain that you were about to scold me, and I am most heartily sick of hearing that I must rest and be careful," she said softly wondering if reminding him of her recent illness was the right thing to say. What did one say when they were in the middle of the street, or upon a doorstep, instead of a ball? If she had a fan in hand, she could use it to say what she could not speak aloud, but of course, she could not do so now. It was not the thing for a woman to flirt in such a setting, and yet, she wanted to do so. "I feel so stifled," she muttered beneath her breath.

"That is just the thing that I have been hoping to hear from you," he replied, surprising her once more, and reaching forward to take her gloved hand. A jolt of pure pleasure strummed through her. He had never touched her before except to check her temperature or see if she was well. This felt very foreign and exciting.

"It is?" She looked at him wide eyes.

"Indeed. There is no better sign of a full recovery than when a patient refuses to think of themselves as ailing any longer. Between that and your healthy color, and the fact that your mother reports that you are sleeping well with none of the tincture I prescribed, I may officially pronounce you to be no longer my patient."

"Thank providence for that," Ellen said fervently, and yet they were back to talking about her illness. How had that happened? "Particularly since there was never really anything actually the matter with me."

"I am forced to disagree with you on that point, madame," he said, "but you will doubtless wish for me to leave it at that, else I am liable to catch myself delivering an academic lecture on the physical affects that can stem from maladies of the spirit ...and I believe that the weight of your basket will not allow you to stand comfortably on the doorstep for so long a monologue," Doctor Larkin said with an unmistakably teasing twinkle. "Besides, I would hate to postpone Thomas' delight at seeing you."

Ellen agreed, and yet, she did not want to end this conversation with Doctor Larkin. "How *is* Thomas doing? Is he getting any stronger?"

"The boy is making great progress, actually. His mother has a natural affinity for nursing the sick, in my opinion. Add to that, she is utterly devoted to her child's care. I doubt Thomas could receive better care if he were to go to the most costly of sanitoriums. The approach of winter has been a concern of mine, but I believe he will not only see next spring but may even be able to revel in it like any other boy."

"But the loss of their cow," Ellen dropped her voice a little lower. "Will that alter your hopeful prediction?"

"It undoubtedly would have, but the animal has already been replaced. In triplicate, as a matter of fact, and accompanied by a rather substantial supply of firewood," the doctor answered, gesturing to a small paddock that lay just beyond the cottage.

Ellen's eyes widened as she noticed for the first time that it was occupied by a trio of sleek Guernsey's who were the very picture of health and contentment as they munched a bale of hay that had been thrown to them with the sparseness of grass at this time of year.

"But that is wonderful. Who?" She raised her eyebrows in question.

"The donor wished to remain anonymous," Doctor Larkin said, his smile deepening. "But I will tell you in confidence that the person in question rides the very finest stallion that I have ever seen in my life."

"Lord Willingham," said Ellen with a nod. "Of course. I ought to have guessed that at once. And doubtless he will never mention a word of it to another soul, even to Arabella. I should like to give her the same hint that you gave me, sir, for although she knows the measure of her betrothed far better than anyone else, it would still give her joy to hear his kindness detailed."

"I will confess that my intention in telling you was that the tale might be carried to Lady Sedgewick's ear," he admitted, taking the basket from Ellen's weary arm in such an automatic gesture that it did not even occur to her to protest.

"Oh, it shall be carried to her straightaway. How I wish that everyone in the village might hear it. I will not disregard his wishes; of course, and besides it is likely for the best that it not be widely known that Edwards has livestock again, at least not until the criminal as identified and stopped. But when I think of how abominably Lord Willingham was treated when he first came here, when he in truth has better character than practically everyone in the village, it really does seem to be a terrible injustice."

"I could not agree with you more. Time and time again Lord Willingham has shown himself to be a gentleman of the highest caliber."

"It is a wonder to me that he did not become bitter and permanently withdrawn as a result of the trials he faced," Ellen reflected. "It would have been impossible to blame him if he had, but instead he seems to embrace his fellow man with boundless enthusiasm."

"Due in some part to his own natural inclination, of course, but I suspect it is the love of Lady Sedgewick that has truly turned the tide. As I said before, it does not do to underestimate the power of the soul or the heart."

There was something at once both sad and hopeful in the young doctor's eyes as he spoke. "Love changes people," he said.

The words suddenly seemed to not be about Lord Willingham and Lady Arabella. Instead, they took on a more intimate tone as his gaze pierced into Ellen, and his words cut to the heart of her. That same heart begin to race as he paused in his speech, and her mouth went dry. She felt none of the cool breeze around them. She felt only the heat of him. The emotion running through her veins was real, as was the warmth of his touch and the closeness of his body to hers.

Her rational mind listed a dozen reasons why she should step away, but her heart whispered that they were meant to be together, and as much as she tried, she didn't know how to silence it. The two of them remained looking at each other for some time, both knowing there was something unspoken between them that was important, but not knowing how to begin to say it or acknowledge what it was that they both felt.

The door opened unexpectedly behind the pair and Mrs. Edwards' voice fell into the silence, breaking the moment. "Why, Doctor Larkin, I had no idea you were still here," she exclaimed. "And Miss Millworth."

"I beg your pardon, I --. Mrs. Edwards." Doctor Larkin regained his composure more quickly than Ellen, who found her sensibilities still reeling. "Miss Millworth arrived just as I was leaving, and I fear I have detained her rather unforgivably," the doctor said, turning to address the thin, pinched-faced woman.

"I'm sure I don't know anything about it being unforgivable, but you ought not stand about any longer in this chilly weather. You must be freezing."

Ellen had not even felt the cold. In fact, she felt rather flushed.

"Won't you come back inside for a spell, Doctor, and warm yourself with a cup of tea? And you, too, Miss Millworth. It is wonderful to see you again. Thomas will be beside himself with happiness," said Mrs. Edwards.

"I have missed our visits terribly," Ellen said, grasping at the new topic, and taking Mrs. Edwards' hand with affection. "I have been interrogating poor Doctor Larkin just now, and I am so glad to hear that Thomas is doing so much better."

"Oh, as am I, Miss Millworth. Sometimes it is all I can do not to cry from happiness at his recovery. Will you come along inside now and see for yourself?"

"With pleasure."

"I believe I will have that cup tea, Mrs. Edwards," said Doctor Larkin who followed her into the house. "If it isn't too much trouble, and then, I can accompany Miss Millworth home."

Ellen's heart gave a giddy little leap at the doctor's words, and she realized she had been hoping rather fervently to continue their conversation. Indeed, he might have gallantly taken the blame for keeping her standing outside the cottage, but she was fairly certain that she had been the one keeping him, and he, undoubtedly had a great many patients to attend.

Telling herself that a cup of tea by the cozy hearth of the cottage would do the overworked doctor a great deal of good, regardless, Ellen firmly turned her attention to little Thomas. The charming child was sitting beside the fire himself, not tucked carefully into a cot as he had been the last time she had seen him. He was still rather too pale and thin, but the dark, bruise-like shadows that had once been beneath his eyes were far less dominant, and his cheeks seemed rounder.

"My goodness, Thomas, you certainly *are* looking stronger," she exclaimed delightedly, crossing to kneel beside the boy.

"Miss Millworth. I have been awfully worried about you," the boy said with candor. "They told me that you have been ill, and I've been saying an extra prayer for you every night."

"Between the prayers inundating heaven, and Doctor Larkin's most excellent care, I don't believe either of us can help but improve. I have missed our visits dreadfully, but to make up for my absence I have brought you *two* books," Ellen said. She had also brought some sweetmeats, a glass jar of strong beef broth, that was canned prior to the poisoning of the sheep, and a snug winter coat, but she knew perfectly well that Thomas considered the books to be the real treasure.

CHAPTER 15

After a delightful half hour of talking and laughing, Ellen left Thomas to rest, which he could only be coaxed to do with her assurance that she would return in a few days' time. Bidding farewell to Mrs. Edwards, she and the doctor exited the cottage together and walked in comfortable silence for a few moments.

"You really have made a world of difference to that child, Miss Millworth," Doctor Larkin said, breaking the silence rather suddenly. "Lifting his spirits as you have done has been vital to his recovery. I wonder if you know the full value of your teaching him to read. It has engaged his mind when his body desperately needed rest and kept him from becoming so fretful and dull that he undoes any progress. I have seen such things become nearly insurmountable obstacles to healing."

"I did not actually set out with the intention of teaching Thomas to read," Ellen confessed, although she was loath to dim the doctor's praise. "He *was* rather cross and restless one day when I was visiting. Mrs. Edwards told me that he had been for several days actually, and she was quite concerned. I happened to have a book with me that day. I planned to call at the Sedgewick's home later and Marianne wanted to borrow a particular translation of The Odyssey from our library."

"Ah, naturally," Doctor Larkin said with a laugh, knowing as well as the rest of the neighborhood how fierce Marianne Sedgewick could become when she had her mind set on a book. "It was brave of you to visit Thomas before her. Any time Miss Sedgewick has requested a volume from me I feel compelled to get it for her immediately if I value life and limb."

Ellen chuckled. "She has been that way for as long as I can recall. It is all the more odd when you consider how perfectly mild and rational she is in all other aspects of her life. Arabella and I have always supposed it to be some sort of result of having such a great intellect."

"A reasonable supposition. But you read the translation to Thomas?" prompted Doctor Larkin.

"Oh, yes, and I am grateful that it *was* a translation, and an actual story besides. Half of the books Marianne pores over are in Greek or some other nastily difficult language, or else great scholarly works that neither Thomas nor myself could comprehend. I was really rather doubtful that he would care for *The Odyssey*, being as young as he is, but he was simply enthralled," Ellen smiled tenderly as she recalled the small boy's rapt fascination that day, as though he had stepped through some invisible doorway.

"I have never met a young boy yet who did not care for *The Odyssey*. It was one of my favorites as a boy," he said, taking Ellen's elbow gently to assist her over a muddy patch of the pathway.

The simple touch, the way he was looking at her with clear admiration, and above all else the focused, interested manner of listening that he had that warmed Ellen's heart. It was as if her every word was a piece of a puzzle he had long been trying to solve. It was funny, she thought helplessly, that she hadn't realized how very cold she felt inside until his smile warmed her.

"Truly?" she said. The thought of Dr. Larkin as a boy filled her heart with a sudden flutter. In her mind's eye she saw a bevy of boys with his same kind eyes and flyaway hair. She paused to take issue with her run-away imagination. She had no right to picture this man's children, considering that he was only her physician, not her beau.

"I think such an adventure lights the imagination of many a boy," Dr. Larkin said.

"I suppose so," she managed to say, keeping her eyes on the path ahead. "I had never particularly cared for the story myself, but reading it to Thomas made me adore it, somehow. Before we knew it a full two hours had passed and Mrs. Edwards almost burnt the bread she was baking that day since she had become caught up in the story as well. When I told Marianne that she could not have the book just yet, it *did* feel rather that I was taking my life into my own hands, but she forgave me for Thomas' sake and even helped me hunt up more stories that he might like. She found several of the Greek myths that he enjoyed."

"Quite merciful of her, really," he said humorously

"Oh, she was like a tigress for a moment or two." Ellen's laugh rang out freely. "But I survived. Thomas began to make it a habit of sitting beside me while I read to him, and I would trace my finger along the words as I read, but from no real design, you know. It was just that it was often late in the afternoon when I visited, and I didn't want to waste the Edwards' candles.

"Holding my finger over my progress helped me to keep my place. I did not know that Thomas was following the reading and looking at the words until much later. I could not visit often enough to please him, although he never complained, but he began poring over the books in my absence, perhaps remembering, or perhaps sounding out the words of the story.

"He would pepper his mother with questions, she told me, and although she has precious little time to sit in idleness, she helped him as often as she could. I did not even know that she could read, but she learned as a child, reading the Bible with her mother."

"They had always hoped that they might be able to send Thomas to school, you know," Doctor Larkin said in his gentle, steady voice. "But when he became ill, they set that dream aside. Edwards had tears in his eyes the day he had Thomas show me that he could read, and I had never once seen him weep, not even when I had to tell him that Thomas was in grave danger and might not survive his illness. He could remain stoic in the face of grief and fear, but pride and hope were more powerful. You gave him that hope, Miss Millworth, gave it to his entire family."

"It wasn't anything half so noble as that," she protested, embarrassed and delighted at the praise, but determined to be perfectly truthful. "The credit really must go to Thomas himself. I did not teach him anything. He absorbed it and puzzled it out for himself."

"We always seem to be disagreeing about the same topic. I assure you that the body cannot thrive when the heart and soul and mind do not. I have seen evidence enough to make me quite certain of that fact."

"Truly?"

"Indeed, I have seen husbands or wives of many years follow their spouses in death, no matter that there is little diagnostically wrong with them. I have seen children fail to thrive when their parents neglect them."

"I suppose that is understandable," Ellen said not wanting to seem contentious.

"It is not always a physical neglect that causes the illness," the doctor explained. "An emotional lack seems to cause the same maladies. We have seen this with soldiers who have lost many friends in battle. It seems to sap their spirit and will to live even when they have managed to avoid the mortal wounds that felled their comrades. They die of minor scrapes, or perhaps of nothing at all, except the guilt that they live when so many are dead.

"I suppose I cannot argue with your expertise," Ellen said.

"Even though you would like to," he laughed, then stopped walking to turn and face her.

"Oh, no, I am a product of your expertise. Never let it be said that I am ungrateful." She grinned at him and his own smile gave way to an expression of such intensity that Ellen caught her breath. "I find it incredibly odd, Miss Millworth, that you are so hasty to devalue the very gifts that you bring to the world. Hope, laughter, beauty and love. They are intangible things, perhaps, but none the less vitally important to us all."

"You are far too kind, sir, and mistaken as well. I do not believe that I devalue the things you have mentioned just now; indeed, quite the opposite. I value them all far too highly to attribute them to myself," she was appalled to find tears springing to her eyes and her voice threatening to waver, yet she seemed unable to release herself from the doctor's steady, passionate gaze.

"It is not kindness to speak the simple truth," he replied gently. "As my patients are often reminding me. I can assure you with my whole heart that I am not uttering idle, baseless flattery when I say that I have always considered you to be a shining example of those virtues —love, life and strength."

"You *know*, perhaps better than anyone else from attending me this past autumn, of my folly and fragility?" A tear slid down Ellen's cheek as she spoke, and she felt a fresh wave of mortification wash over her, but she lifted her chin, determined to speak aloud the thought that had been secretly tormenting her, but somehow, she could not. His very nearness stole her breath and thus the words stuck in her throat.

"Miss Millworth, I can assure you that my admiration and esteem for you has not once faltered or diminished. Indeed, it has only grown by such leaps and bounds that I cannot seem to help but express it," Doctor Larkin murmured, reaching out to trace away the tear glistening in the late morning sunlight with his finger.

Ellen felt such a thrill at the gesture and the undeniable sincerity in the doctor's declaration that her heart seemed to jump in her chest and migrate to her throat where it stuck with thudding impropriety. Almost imperceptibly he angled his head in such a way that she was certain that he was going to kiss her, and she could think of nothing in the world she wanted more. Without any conscious intention, she took an encouraging step closer.

"Doctor Larkin." the urgent shout startled Ellen more thoroughly than a booming thunderclap could have, and she jolted back away from the doctor, a feeling of embarrassment welling up and coloring her face. Her body seemed to be trembling all over in a rush of excitement or perhaps it was the chilly air. Yes. She would blame her trembling on the weather.

Running frantically up the muddy track was a gangling youth whom Ellen recognized as a servant from Lady Evans' estate. Her heart racing and her face aflame, she turned away in confusion for a moment, in an attempt to regain her composure. What had she been thinking? She wondered furiously. Throwing both caution and propriety to the winds with scarcely a second thought. Had she not learned from her previous, disastrous connection that such behavior was pure folly. It was maddening to realize how quickly she could forget those hard lessons and abandon them for a rush of emotions.

"Gerald?" Doctor Larkin replied in an admirably composed voice, although he also took a step back, giving Ellen room to breathe. "Whatever is the matter?"

"I've been looking for you for a quarter of an hour at least, sir," the boy panted, coming to an ungraceful halt in the mud before them. "Your housekeeper said she thought you were calling at Edwards' cottage, but she expected you back before now. It's Lady Evans, she's been taken dreadfully ill, sir, and I was told to bring you to her at once."

"Certainly, lad, I will make all possible haste—" the doctor began, then seemed to recall his companion. "Miss Millworth, I regret very much the necessity of cutting short our conversation. I have every hope that we may continue it at a later time, if you are able to pardon my abrupt departure."

"Of course, you must go at once," Ellen said quickly, doing her best to quash the flutter in her heart that his expression caused. "You need not wait for me, I walked this way by myself and besides, we are more than halfway back to my home. Go and see to poor Lady Evans. Go." she added, with a shaky laugh, as she saw that he still seemed torn.

With a hasty bow, Doctor Larkin turned and rushed away to attend to matters of life and death, leaving Ellen to walk slowly home, her progress hindered by her confused whirl of thoughts and emotions.

Hours later, the joy and hope that he had felt during his interlude with Ellen a distant and faintly surreal memory, Doctor Roger Larkin dropped to a chair in his disordered office. He was far too exhausted to even look at the meal that had been left out for him by the housekeeper. It had grown stone cold anyhow. Even more profound than the toll taken by strenuous hours spent in the attempt to save Lady Evans' life, he was utterly depleted by the nagging sense of failure that haunted him every time he lost a patient.

It was all very well to say that every doctor would inevitably lose the battle with death on quite a few occasions and that a good physician must be able to accept that fact and instead think of the many lives saved. Roger knew it to be true and reasonable, and yet in his very soul he could not help but despise each and every defeat.

Particularly in such a case as this, where the patient was hale and hearty and by all rights ought to have gone on barking orders and feuding with her neighbors for another decade at the least. Still worse, Lady Evans had not met with an untimely accident or sudden illness. Rather, Roger knew, she had been deliberately cut down by her fellow man. She had been poisoned. It was no longer sheep and cows who were being poisoned, but a human being. He struggled to believe that it was a horrible accident. Perhaps she ate one of the tainted animals, but he had warned the village and the way gossip flew, he could not believe that Lady Evans was unaware of the situation. No. He could not help but think that the livestock were only a smoke screen to hide the true act of depravity, the murder of another human being.

CHAPTER 16

Ellen sat with her parents in the parlor the next morning, the cheery fire that danced in the hearth doing precious little to dispel the somber mood that hung over them both. She had feared that the doctor would make good on his promise to continue their conversation later in the afternoon of the previous day, and if he did, she could not think of what she might say to him. One steady, soul-searching look from the man and all sense seemed to flee directly out of her, replaced with sheer emotion. He was certainly the very last person she ought to speak to if she were to have a hope of staying true to her resolve of keeping her feelings in check.

Unreasonably, she had been terribly disappointed when Doctor Larkin had *not* come to call on her after all, which really, she reflected wearily, was yet another proof that her heart was an unreliable guide, at best. Later that evening, when news had come of Lady Evans' sudden death, the doctor's absence was easy to understand. Ellen had tortured herself a little by picturing him sad and weary, without a comforting home to take solace in, only that dismally untidy house that wanted so badly to be taken in hand. It had been a rather thrilling flight of fancy to allow herself, if only for a quarter of an hour, to envision herself as the one to do it. The fine, if neglected, old lodge could be made a welcoming, cheerful home that the doctor would be happy to return to after even the most miserable of days. The thought of being there to lift his spirits and fuss over him just a little was so enticing that Ellen had been aghast to realize how much she wanted just that. She chided herself that she was thinking of some romantic interlude, when a woman was dead. Whatever was wrong with her?

Her face heated a bit to recall her thoughts the next morning, but fortunately her seat was close enough beside the fire to explain away the rosy glow easily. One caller after another had come by that morning, a dreary procession of people wishing to discuss the death of Lady Evans and glean any new information that Mrs. Millworth might possess.

Their most recent visitor had only just departed, leaving Ellen with the unpleasant impression that the worst of dying might just be the incessant discussion of one's character, veiled unconvincingly with a pretense of gloom.

"That was the worst one so far," she commented to her mother in an aggrieved voice. "And you know perfectly well that Mrs. Creswick never cared for Lady Evans whatsoever."

"I won't deny it was Ier dreadful, dearest, but-" Mrs. Millworth was cut short by the announcement that Doctor Larkin had come to call. She concluded whatever charitable explanation she had been about for the transparently gleeful Mrs. Creswick, but Ellen did not hear a word of the explanation since her heart was pounding so hard it drowned out all other sound.

"Mrs. Millworth, Miss Millworth," the doctor said with a bow as he entered the cozy parlor. He *did* look pitiably haggard and pale, Ellen noticed at once, yearning to comfort him somehow.

"Dear me, Doctor Larkin, you look as thought you had not slept a wink." exclaimed Mrs. Millworth speaking the words that expressed her daughter's feelings.

"Perhaps just that much, but scarcely more," he replied with only a bare shadow of his usual gentle humor. "I have been too greatly disturbed to rest much. As a matter of fact, it is most likely rather thoughtless of me to come here now, when my thoughts are bleak and the sharing of them I in no way provide a solution."

"Nonsense," Mrs. Millworth said in a briskly maternal tone. "Many matters can only be truly understood if they have been examined and discussed with trusted companions. I should be quite gratified for you to consider us as such, for your own sake as much as for the sake of my friendship with your mother."

"That is precisely my feelings as well," added in Mr. Millworth with a warm approving smile at his wife. "Come, sit down and unburden yourself at once if you feel it might help you clarify your thoughts."

"Thank you," Doctor Larkin said simply, but with heartfelt sincerity. He took the seat that Mr. Millworth had indicated, directly across from Ellen, and his eyes fixed upon hers for a brief moment in a way that made her feel quite certain that he intended to further pursue what had been interrupted the day before even if the present was not the time for such matters.

"I daresay this has something to do with the unfortunate death of Lady Evans," Mr. Millworth said encouragingly. "The news came as quite a surprise to us. She has always been so fiercely healthy; I suppose I should term it."

"That is certainly a more charitable phrase than most that we have heard employed in Lady Evans' description this morning," said Mrs. Millworth with a gentle smile. "But for all that she was so imperious and opinionated, I always rather liked her. Behind all of her bluster and demands she was quite a good-hearted woman."

"My thoughts on her have been similar ever since I came to this village," Doctor Larkin agreed, rubbing a strong, skilled hand over his face in a weary gesture. "But at least one person has disagreed with that assessment of Lady Evans' character enough to end her life."

"You don't mean to say that the poor woman was murdered." The horrified words burst out of Ellen as she had forgotten her confusion and shyness in the doctor's presence. "I thought she had been taken ill. I had not thought—"

"Yes," the doctor nodded. "I am afraid that she *was* murdered. And moreover, her death was caused by the same type of poison that has been used to kill all the livestock recently. Our culprit, whoever he may be, has evidently decided to move on from animals and begin assassinating humans."

"You feared all along that something of this nature might happen, although you did not say it in so many words," Mr. Millworth reflected, his tone and manner grave.

"I did, although I was loathed to speak it. Indeed, I hoped I was mistaken in my suspicion. Attempting to follow the logic of a disordered mind, though, this manner of escalation seemed likely. If we could have discovered and apprehended the culprit soon enough, we might have spared Lady Evans' life, and the culprit's as well. His fate was sealed along with hers the moment that she took the first sip of brandy."

"The poison was mixed with brandy?" asked Mr. Millworth with a frown. "You are quite certain?"

"Perfectly certain. There can be no doubt about it. The remnants of the drink were still in her glass, and my tests showed vast quantities of the poison present in both the glass and the bottle of brandy. It was enough to have killed the poor woman ten times over, in my opinion. There was no question of saving her life, I am afraid, only of doing what little I could to ease her suffering."

"Would…would it have made much of a difference if you had been able to see to her sooner?" Ellen forced herself to ask the question that had been haunting her conscience since the news of Lady Evans' death had been brought to them the night before. The doctor would not have been so difficult to locate if he had not tarried at the cottage in order to walk her home. The idea that she might have inadvertently played a part in someone's death was almost too horrifying to contemplate.

Doctor Larkin shook his head firmly, apparently understanding the reason for her question.

"No, it really would have made no difference at all, unless I had been standing by her side the moment that she set her lips to the glass and kept her from downing such a large swallow. An aqueous solution of ammonia salts or hartshorn, if administered *very* promptly, has sometimes proven to be an effective antidote to laurel water if the dosage is small. But even if I had been immediately on hand, there would have been barely a chance of saving Lady Evans. As I said, there was a massive amount of laurel water mixed into the brandy. I suppose our killer knows more about how much of the poison will be required to kill a cow or an ox and did not think to vary the amount for a small, elderly woman."

"It is a wonder that Lady Evans did not notice a difference in the taste and smell of the brandy. Although, I cannot imagine why she would be drinking brandy at all at such an hour of the day," mused Mrs. Millworth, quite oblivious to Ellen's soft sigh of relief at the doctor's words.

"It seems to be a particularly strong bottle of cherry-flavored brandy," he explained. "The taste and smell of the toxin would have been masked, and as it appeared to be a new bottle. I do not believe she attributed anything unusual, or did not notice due to the cherry flavoring. As for your second point, Lady Evans was in the habit of taking a glass of brandy now and then to calm her nerves. The time of day would have made little difference to her if she were sufficiently upset about something."

"Calm her nerves indeed," Mother replied. "I should not speak ill of the dead, but I have rarely known anyone else who so greatly enjoyed being outraged and giving a piece of her mind to friends, acquaintances, and strangers alike. I never so much as suspected that she *had* nerves."

"You are quite right," the doctor agreed with a reluctant smile. "Many interactions that might reasonably be expected to cause distress had no negative effect upon Lady Evans. Indeed, she seemed to find arguments and conflict rather invigorating, as you say. But she *did* have deeply sensitive feelings. Surprisingly sensitive feelings on several matters and could be wounded and distraught quite unexpectedly."

"I suppose I can imagine that easily enough," Mrs. Millworth murmured thoughtfully. "Often you *do* find it to be the case that the more a person prides themselves on speaking their mind, the less they care to have anyone else speak *theirs*. But regardless of all that, the poor woman hardly deserved such a fate as this. If only that wretch Marksham had not buried his head so obstinately in the sand about the poisoning of the livestock, the murderer might have been apprehended well before now. It is unfair and uncharitable of me, I am sure, but I cannot help but feel that Mr. Marksham is a little bit to blame."

"Whether it is unfair and uncharitable, I do not know, but I feel just the same way," said Doctor Larkin, some of the weariness returning to his voice as he rose from his seat with evident reluctance. "But regardless of that, I think it is my duty to inform Mr. Marksham, in his official capacity as magistrate, that the death of Lady Evans was caused deliberately and must be investigated as a crime. I cannot claim that I am looking forward to such a conversation, but it must be done nevertheless, and I had best not put it off any longer."

"If you mean to go speak to him directly, then I believe I had better call on Lord Sedgewick and perhaps some others at once. You might mention that to Marksham when you meet with him. I am sure he is quite capable of dismissing the whole matter without a second thought, unless he knows that the rest of the gentry hereabouts are demanding a proper investigation," Mr. Millworth decided.

"He will make a sad muddle of any investigation, regardless of how much he might feel pressed. Really, I cannot think of a man who is less qualified to be a magistrate," his wife said, shaking her head.

"I will go with you, Papa, I wanted to call on Arabella today." An idea had presented itself to Ellen as her mother had been speaking, and impulsively, she wanted to pursue it without any further hesitation.

PART III

CHAPTER 17

"It is rather soon to pay our condolences to Miss Stanton," Arabella complained, not for the first time since Ellen had arrived and insisted that they make a call at Tidwell House. "Even if, as you said before, she might be in need of some assistance with the arrangements. Although, I suppose it is all terribly overwhelming, and she has been kept down so by Lady Evans that it may be difficult for her to know how to take charge of things all at once."

"That isn't *precisely* why I want to make a call so urgently," confessed Ellen in a sheepish tone. "Although I am certain that Miss Stanton will be feeling at least a little lost and bewildered just now. I could not say my real reason earlier, or else your sisters would be sure to insist upon coming with us."

"That is entirely likely," laughed Arabella. "I *thought* you were trying to give me a meaningful look when I didn't agree at once to leave, which is why I acquiesced even though I was hoping to overhear what the gentlemen might have to say in regard to the investigation. What is your true purpose, then?"

"I want to take part in the investigation myself, as a matter of fact. Mr. Marksham is far too arrogant and stupid to find out any fact that doesn't immediately announce itself to him. Even then, he is perfectly capable of ignoring a fact if he doesn't care for it. Of course, I have no doubt the gentlemen will not leave such a serious matter entirely in Mr. Marksham's hands. Doctor Larkin is sure to pursue the truth, for one."

"However?" Arabella prompted when Ellen fell silent for a moment.

Ellen blushed, flustered by how rapidly she had lost her train of thought in contemplating the doctor's weary determination, such an odd thing to find fascinating.

"However, I don't know that the gentlemen, any of them, are the best suited for discovering what really happened to Lady Evans. People see them as authorities and may keep details to themselves for fear of looking foolish, or fear of seeming to make an accusation against the wrong person. As women, I think we can investigate far more effectively. *I* am not likely to put anyone on their guard, nor are you, and it occurred to me that it would be the most natural thing in the world if we were to run over to Tidwell House to pay our condolences to Miss Stanton and offer our support and assistance."

"Seeing as she is quite alone in the world now," Arabella nodded, comprehending the idea perfectly. "And she is more likely to be comfortable speaking to ladies close to her own age. There is no harm in it, even if it happens to come to nothing, it is a kindness, and you are quite right that we *may* uncover something that any number of gentlemen cannot."

"I am glad that you see the sense in my idea, although I have no doubt that you would go along with me even if you thought the entire errand was a waste of time," said Ellen with a dimpling smile.

"That is indeed the truth, and one of the marvelous things about having such a lifelong friendship as ours. Of course, the downside of such a connection is that as your lifelong companion I cannot fail to notice certain telling things in your manner, Miss Ellen Millworth."

"My manner?" Ellen was genuinely baffled at the comment.

"Mmm, indeed yes. You blushed quite crimson just now when you mentioned a certain doctor of our acquaintance and his noble and relentless pursuit of the truth," Arabella said rather archly, with a sidelong glance at her friend.

"I certainly never said any such thing as a noble and relentless pursuit of the truth," protested Ellen, although she could feel her face heat once again.

"Oh, not out loud," conceded Arabella airily, waving off the objection. "The noble and relentless bit was strongly implied, if unspoken. But your blush was unmistakable, as was your confusion and abstraction after you mentioned him. You cannot mean to tell me that I am mistaken, dearest."

"I *wish* you were mistaken. I wish it most heartily," Ellen sighed, dispirited. "I have been fighting against my ridiculous feelings for Doctor Larkin for weeks, although it seems like years."

"But why? If you care for him, I cannot imagine any impediment worth such an extended struggle."

"You are a truly loyal, and perhaps blindly affectionate friend, to not even entertain the notion that someone I admire, might not necessarily care for me."

"I make a point of not entertaining ridiculous notions," Arabella laughed. "As if any gentleman in existence could help but find you the most lovely and charming of creatures. But none of those abstract gentlemen are the point just now, we are speaking of Doctor Larkin, and I have noticed how he looks at you. There is certainly no chance of your feelings being unreciprocated."

"I do not feel half so certain as you seem to be," returned Ellen moodily. "I cannot trust my feelings as I am sure you know. Sometimes I think that perhaps he *might* care a little. Other times I am certain such an idea is sheer folly, to say nothing of self-conceit. He is merely as sympathetic and solicitous towards me as he is to any of his patients. But that is hardly the primary obstacle."

"Well, then, what *is*?" Arabella paused, tapping her foot and demanded An explanation after waiting a very brief moment.

"Why, I am." exclaimed Ellen, the words bursting passionately from her in a sudden tempest of emotion. "How can I ever trust my heart to steer me right, after following it made me such an utter fool? My admiration for a gentleman has clearly been proven to be no sure indication of his worth, as you well know. Of all people, Arabella, *you* should know how impossible my behavior was when I was in love, throwing decorum and caution to the wind quite willfully, agreeing to a clandestine correspondence when, of course, I knew it to be wrong. All the blame cannot rest on Sir Randall, there is something wrong with me as well."

"Oh no, dear," Arabella said, but Ellen shook her head. "Why, yesterday when Doctor Larkin almost kissed me, I had every intention of letting him. As if I had learned nothing from past experiences, as if I were eager to be mad once more. He is a selfless man and deserves far better than a silly, emotional idiot such as myself. I cannot allow—"

The two girls stopped walking, pausing on the path to face one another. Ellen concluded her bitter speech feeling rather wild, tears escaping her eyes unheeded, her breath coming in ragged gasps as the pent-up storm forced its way out of her. Arabella, on the other hand, remained perfectly calm and surveyed her friend with a steady, contemplative gaze. "He almost kissed you?" she repeated.

Ellen blushed prettily, but said nothing to negate the fact.

"I have listened to you wax poetic about the wonders of the despicable Sir James, for what seemed at the time to be an eternity," she finally said, unexpectedly and unsympathetically. "Because I love you dearly and because I knew that if I breathed a word of criticism or doubt that I would have no chance of helping you gain free of the man. But I may say with a perfectly clear conscience that until today I have never heard you utter such complete nonsense as this. *You cannot allow?*"

"Arabella," Ellen gasped, stung.

"You *have* insisted of late that we ought not continue shielding you from unpleasant things," pointed out Arabella, and Ellen was forced to nod in agreement, even if she wished her friend had not taken her quite so thoroughly at her word.

"That is true."

"So step back for one moment and attempt to really hear yourself. Why, half of what you said just now is in direct opposition to the other half. The doctor almost kissed you, but it is only self-conceit that makes you think he might care for you? Then you state that your admiration for a gentleman is no indication of his character, and that Dr. Larkin is a wonderful man who deserves a far better wife than yourself. It is all rank folly if taken together, for those things cannot be all true at the same time. Let us remember you did not initiate the kiss." Arabella raised a curious eyebrow. "Or did you?"

"Of course not," Ellen said mortified.

"And so, this thought that he does admire you cannot be solely in your imagination. A man such as Dr. Larkin does not go about kissing young women indiscriminately, does he?"

"Well, no," Ellen whispered.

"Then, it is clear he has some regard for you."

"I didn't think of that," Ellen admitted, struck by Arabella's statement.

"Ellen, when my family returned from Bath, I had made up my mind that as I had not fallen in love with any acceptable gentleman, I would simply select the worthiest candidate and marry him without caring for him. Imagine if I had done that. I might very well be engaged to some hopelessly dull fop instead of the dearest, most perfectly suited man in existence." Arabella gave a delicate shudder at the idea.

"He *is* rather perfectly suited for you," agreed Ellen with a small smile. "Although certainly not the impeccable sort of gentleman that you were once so determined to wed."

"Not in the least – why, I would never have given him the most fleeting moment of thought if I had not needed his assistance in saving you from that villain. First, I thought he was of lower birth, but even if he had been, he is a wonderful man, and I would not want any other by my side. A duke or the Regent himself would not be a better choice."

"The Regent," scoffed Ellen, shivering as she thought of the fat indulgent prince, "is no catch."

"I suppose so," Arabella agreed, "But the point is, by narrow-mindedly restricting myself to one foolish idea I would have missed my only opportunity for real, lifelong love and companionship. Helping you, saved me from that, dearest, and I am quite indebted to you."

"I don't see how, not even remotely. If I hadn't been so silly and empty-headed, I might have saved everyone a great deal of trouble, yourself included."

"I have learned, barely, I'll grant you, but I *have* learned that saving people from too much trouble only hinders their growth," Arabella countered gently. "Consider my sisters, or even myself. I was miserably unhappy, you know, but I had made my mind up to do my duty. Helping you felt like something of a reprieve although I would not have been able to see it clearly as such at the time. I want you to know, I was quite vexed with you."

Ellen stared at her friend in frank astonishment since she had never considered the matter from her friend's point of view.

"I cannot decide if I am more amazed at the idea of your being miserably unhappy and hiding it so well, or the idea that my selfish actions could possibly have had a positive effect on anything," she ventured after a moment.

"Providence does not make errors," Arabella said. "At the risk of sounding pedantic, we are where we find ourselves for a reason. You and I are no different."

"I am sure we are," Ellen argued.

"I shall add to your dilemma and shock you further by confessing that I was also quite envious of you," Arabella replied, laughing at the expression on Ellen's face. "I was. Your ability to love so deeply and entirely has always been a quality that I wished to see in myself. The capacity to love so fully and unconditionally is such a beautiful thing. You must not let that scoundrel take it from you. The love was not returned, but you loved, nonetheless, deeply and without reserve and that is a grand thing. Love is never in vain. You must not allow yourself to be limited by a foolish, self-imposed rule as I almost did."

"Is that what I am doing?" Ellen mused, struck by the idea.

"It's something to consider. In the meantime, you can explain to me just exactly what you meant when you said that he almost kissed you."

Ellen felt her spirits lift as she laughed with her dearest friend and it felt wonderfully freeing, to laugh at last. She launched into a lively description of the interaction. If Arabella did not think that she ought to quell her feelings for Doctor Larkin, then perhaps she could permit herself to hope and dream a little bit. The day seemed suddenly brighter and more lovely than it had just a moment ago, despite their grim errand.

CHAPTER 18

The mood in the Tidwell House was somehow both somber and disordered when the two young ladies arrived and apologetically explained the reason for their visit. Lady Evans's longtime housekeeper seemed faintly scandalized at the breach of protocol, but dutifully relayed their arrival to Miss Stanton, who agreed to see them at once.

Garbed in black, her face drawn and her eyes red from recent weeping, the mousy young woman seemed as subdued as ever when she received her visitors in a rather stuffy parlor.

"I hope you will forgive our calling on you at such a time," Arabella began once they had been seated and exchanged greetings. "It isn't quite regular, I know, but we felt you might welcome a little assistance with things, being alone in the world as you are."

"You've had such a dreadful shock, and it must be rather overwhelming for you, with no one else here to share your grief," Ellen added, her sympathy quite genuine as she surveyed Miss Stanton. The young woman had always been so cowed and quiet in the presence of her overbearing aunt, yet she seemed perfectly lost without the woman.

"That is nice of you to say so," Miss Stanton murmured, her eyes glancing from Arabella to Ellen uncertainly. "I am rather surprised that you thought of me. Well, that is to say, not *you* specifically. No, I did not mean that. I meant only to say that I am surprised that anyone would have thought of... you are both very kind," she concluded lamely, flushing scarlet and looking so miserably confused and awkward that Ellen's heart went completely out to her.

"Not at all," she replied briskly, determined to set Miss Stanton at ease and bridge the uncomfortable lapse in conversation before it could grow any longer. "I know perhaps it may not seem as if there is much that we can do, but sometimes simply having a friend or two to listen can be quite helpful. We both regret that we have not been more persistent in our efforts to get to know you sooner, Miss Stanton."

"It is true," Arabella agreed, prepared to stretch the truth a little if needed. "I thought just that when you came to my aid so heroically at my father's dinner party recently. It was perfectly marvelous, the way you were able to put together such a splendid evening of music with so little notice."

"Oh, I was very happy to do it," Miss Stanton said, flushing scarlet once again, this time from pleasure at the attention and compliments. "I am always glad to give assistance where I can, and besides that I do so love to play."

"That is no small wonder, with a talent such as yours. And now you must allow me to repay the favor if possible and tell me if there is any assistance that Ellen or myself could provide to you."

"I hardly even know. I must confess that I find myself still half waiting for my aunt to sweep in and tell me exactly what I ought to be doing, and how I ought to do it."

"And change her mind half a dozen times, as likely as not," Ellen suggested with a friendly smile, which Miss Stanton returned after looking rather startled for a moment.

"That is just the sort of thing she would do," she agreed with half a laugh. "And never give the slightest indication that there had been any inconsistency, whatsoever."

"I once heard an unfortunate visiting clergyman protest when she scolded him for the content of his sermon. Yet, he had done nothing but follow her own suggestion of two days prior. Her outrage on that occasion was really rather spectacular, and I do not believe that anyone dared to suggest such a thing since then," said Arabella with a slight smile. "She was without a doubt, like no other."

"Yes…That must have happened before I came to stay here, but it does sound perfectly like her. But she really was a wonderful woman, I hope I have not given the impression to either of you that I am ungrateful to her," said Miss Stanton hastily.

"I think it is possible to love and appreciate someone, while still noticing their little foibles," Ellen reassured the woman. "Indeed, one would need to be both deaf and blind to keep from noticing in most cases. And I am certain that as generous as your aunt was to you, your companionship was very valuable to her as well."

"Generous?" the lady said, her complexion pale.

"Why yes. I am certain I heard her singing your praises a time or two."

Miss Stanton cleared her throat and looked shyly at the floor. "Of course, you meant…I mean, I hope so. Ever since I came to stay here, I have always done my best to make myself useful in any way that I could, although I know my aunt was often terribly vexed with my shyness and dullness in company. I hope she knows now that I really did try my best to improve."

A series of tears slid down Miss Stanton's pale cheek, and she gazed downwards at her clasped hands for a moment, as if gathering her composure. Ellen was struck suddenly by just how dreary the girl's existence had been in her time at Tidwell House, if girl was really the correct term. Miss Stanton looked to be much closer to twenty-five or more, and any faint prettiness she might have once possessed seemed to have already begun to fade.

"I am certain that she knows now and hopes that you find happiness in the future," Arabella murmured. "Have you any other family?"

"No, my aunt was the only living relative that I had, once my mother died. And Mother, *she* was Aunt Agatha's niece, you know, I am only her great-niece. Well, Mother fell out with Aunt Agatha years ago. Long before I was born, in fact, because Aunt Agatha did not approve of Mother's marriage. Mother was far too proud to consider writing and asking for help when my father died, although I daresay that was foolish of her since he had spent the majority of her income and left us with very little to live on after his death. I was only fifteen at the time, and the change in our circumstances was rather bewildering to me. I had thought I would have a season, however small, and then there was nothing."

"How dreadful," said Ellen. It was not difficult by any means to picture Mary Stanton resignedly watching the brightest parts of girlhood slip away in the struggle of a genteel poverty. It seemed quite tragic to think of.

"It is disloyal to my father, I suppose, to say that really my aunt was rather correct in her original assessment of his suitability, and it hurt my feelings to hear *her* say it so frequently after I came here. But I cannot deny the truth of it," Miss Stanton continued. "It was likewise rather disloyal to my mother for me to come here at all. She made it quite clear that her dying wish was that I would continue her grudge against Aunt Agatha. But I really could not think of what else to do or who else I might turn to, so I wrote to my aunt and explained the difficulty in which I found myself, and she sent for me at once."

"She had a very generous heart beneath all of her bluster; my mother was only just saying that this morning when we were discussing the terrible news."

"That is entirely accurate, and she was a compassionate soul as well." Miss Stanton seemed to gain her footing and continued on apace. "She was ever concerned with others well-being, and if she ever said a hurtful thing it was not with the intention of causing pain. Indeed, she believed wholeheartedly that it was her duty to speak her mind. Perhaps it was her duty. She certainly gave a great deal of good advice and guidance. I really do not know what I shall do without her, and I am more alone than ever now. It has lifted my spirits more than either of you might imagine, that you have shown such compassion in coming here today," Miss Stanton said, pressing her lips together firmly as if to keep them from trembling.

Ellen felt a pang of guilt as she remembered that their purpose in calling at Tidwell House had not been motivated entirely by empathy for the woman's grief. Exchanging a glance with Arabella when Miss Stanton retired for a moment behind her handkerchief, she could see that her friend was feeling just the same way. It couldn't be helped, she decided resolutely. Besides, they had an ulterior motive did not necessarily cancel out any good that they might accomplish, particularly if they continued to befriend the unfortunate Mary Stanton in the future, an intention Ellen could see plainly mirrored in Arabella's eyes.

"It is a great relief that you do not feel our visit is an intrusion," she said, resolutely putting her guilty conscience aside for the time being. "I hope you will not be offended if I ask, although it could also be seen as an intrusion, but surely you are not quite so bereft as before, are you? I mean, surely Lady Evans has provided for your future, hasn't she? I do not mean to be impertinent; I assure you, only, perhaps we could in some way, be helpful."

"Oh, pray do not worry yourself on that account, I am quite honored by your interest," Miss Stanton replied, setting her crumpled handkerchief aside and gazing at Ellen with an expression of great earnestness. "And you are right to guess that my aunt has provided quite generously for my future. In fact, her solicitor was here only last week, and Aunt Agatha was perfectly clear in her instructions to him that I was to be her sole beneficiary. That ought not to have come to pass for years and years. It seemed so abstract and far away that I scarcely gave it a moment's thought at the time. But now I suppose I shall have to send for the solicitor and the poor man will have to make the journey here from London all over again. It seems most inconvenient for him, but then he was quite accustomed to visiting Tidwell House rather frequently. Aunt Agatha would send for him whenever the whim struck her, and I suppose he knew it was best to heed her wishes promptly. Oh, I assure you that I do not intend to make her sound so tyrannical, yet it keeps happening. I should keep my mouth shut, as I have always done. I have always had such a terrible difficulty in expressing myself correctly."

"No, indeed, we understand. There is no need to distress yourself. You may speak freely before us and not worry that we are eager to carry gossip or innuendoes about," reassured Arabella. "I assure you, Miss Millworth and myself have both been the subject of such discussions and would never dream of subjecting anyone else to such treatment. After all, you must know I am engaged to marry Lord Willingham, who was recently the brunt of much gossip."

Ellen nodded. "Gossip is as gossip does," she said with a shake of her head. "You must pay it no mind."

"Thank you, Miss Millworth. Lady Sedgewick," Miss Stanton sniffled and smiled, looking like a timid child who has been offered a sweet. "I cannot say what that means to me. And truly, Aunt Agatha was not quite frivolous in demanding the attendance of her solicitor. There seems to have been some sort of a dispute with a neighbor, Mr. Marksham, I believe it was. It has dragged on for years and years. I do not really comprehend the details of it. The matter always put my poor aunt into such a bad humor that I never asked for clarification. But a great deal of legal advice *did* seem to be required, and certainly I never heard the solicitor complain."

"Oh, yes, I have heard my parents discussing their feud since I was quite a small child," Ellen said. "Something about the boundaries between the two estates, I believe. I do hope that *you* will not be troubled by him on that front, especially at such a distressing time as this. But you may have already gathered that Mr. Marksham can be a rather difficult sort of person."

"To put it delicately," agreed Arabella with a little laugh. "But you must tell us if he attempts to bully you over the matter, Miss Stanton. You saw how your aunt stood up to him the other day and refused to be cowed. I daresay that is half of the reason the two of them had such difficulties in resolving their dispute, for his vanity does not seem to permit much dissent, particularly from a lady. I rather suspect that he will imagine that he can order you about with more success than he could ever find with Lady Evans."

"I have always been hopeless at standing up for myself, I am afraid," admitted Miss Stanton. "Perhaps your friendships will help me learn to be more valiant, but fortunately I do not believe that I will have any trouble with Mr. Marksham. He and Aunt Agatha seemed to have settled their dispute once and for all, not two days ago. It is nice to think that she can rest easy on that account, particularly since she got the better of him from what I understood. Why, he not only came here to apologize quite humbly, but he also brought the most thoughtful gift. A peace offering, he called it, a lovely bottle of brandy that he said would suit her perfectly. He had evidently taken a great deal of care in selecting just the right one, and my aunt was quite pleased by it. How sad to think that she never even had a chance to taste it."

CHAPTER 19

Ellen narrowly restrained her gasp of horror at Miss Stanton's off-handed statement, and she saw out of the corner of her eye that Arabella's posture had gone suddenly tense and rigid. She did not dare look at her friend, and she was certain that her own manner must show the shock that she was feeling, but fortunately Miss Stanton did not seem to notice. She was gazing rather dreamily at the fire that danced in the parlor hearth, twisting her much-abused handkerchief idly, and reflecting on her great-aunt's life in a soft voice.

Doctor Larkin had been perfectly certain that the poison had been concealed in the brandy that Lady Evans had taken, and Ellen knew he would not make a claim like that if there had been any doubt. Surely it could not be a coincidence that the magistrate had gifted Lady Evans with a bottle of brandy so soon before her death.

Indeed, she thought, the fact that he had given his long-time foe a gift and an apology was highly suspicious. Voluntarily admitting wrongdoing and making amends was so uncharacteristic of Mr. Marksham that Lady Evans really ought to have guessed at his ill intentions. And no wonder he had been so dismissive and stubborn about the deaths of the livestock. It all lined up so neatly in a row, and in such an unexpected, and yet logical manner, that Ellen felt as if she must jump up from her chair and rush to the village to demand the magistrate's arrest without wasting another moment.

Rather than give into that impulse, however, she took a few deep breaths to compose herself, and spoke when she was certain that her voice would be steady and calm. It would not do to leap to conclusions and upset poor Miss Stanton with wild accusations, particularly if they happened to be unfounded. After all, the girl had said that her aunt *hadn't* even tasted the brandy before her death, so perhaps the poison had been in a different bottle.

"Were you with your aunt when she took ill yesterday?" she asked gently as soon as there was a reasonable pause in Miss Stanton's tearful ruminations.

"I? No, I wasn't. Isn't that terrible? She was all alone, the poor woman, and I was not even there to help or comfort her. Ordinarily she feels tired around midday and takes a rest, and my presence is not needed for at least an hour, so I have gotten into the habit of taking a walk on the grounds when she retires to her boudoir. I do not think I was gone any longer than usual, but by the time I returned the entire household was in an uproar and the doctor had already been sent for. She was quite beyond speech, and I will never even know if she was able to hear my pleading or my farewells."

"I am sure that she still knew, in her heart, that you were there with her at the end, dear," said Arabella, her voice also steady as she had recovered her own composure.

"It was all so dreadfully sudden and unexpected," Miss Stanton said plaintively, shaking her head in sorrow. "I have been trying all morning to remember just what the last thing was that I said to her before she retired to her boudoir, but it has proven to be a futile effort. I probably made some meaningless, inconsequential remark about the weather or something of that trivial nature. She was not scolding me, so that is something I may hold on to. She was so often annoyed with me, but at least I didn't annoy her at the last."

"Of course, you didn't," soothed Arabella. "I believe she was quite happy with you, and I know she was ever so proud of your talent with music, you know. She told me so herself when you were playing the harp for us."

"Did she really?" The lady was pale. She seemed quite stricken with the thought. Perhaps, she was just coming to terms with the fact that her only relative was gone now, Ellen thought. She could not imagine how she would feel if her dear parents passed, and yet she knew they would likely die before she. Please God, she prayed silently, let it be many years yet before I lose my parents.

As an only child, they were very precious to her. She thought of the times she had argued with her own mother, like any child did, and the notion was like a wound in her heart. She felt tears well as she imagined that Miss Stanton must feel much the same way about her own aunt, even if they did not always get along. In some ways, such a thing was more grievous, since there was now no way to heal any rift in the relationship.

"Oh yes, indeed she said that she had never known a more accomplished musician, and that your talent was a credit to your breeding," Arabella said brightly.

Ellen pulled herself from her musings.

"Thank you so much for telling me that," the girl said in a choked voice, her pale skin flushing once more. "Aunt Agnes was not inclined to effusive compliments, you know, so it means a great deal to hear that she felt that way."

"I imagine you will hear many more examples of her praises for you in the days to come, as everyone else comes to pay their condolences," said Ellen. "But we must not keep you any longer just now, even though you are too polite to say how weary you must be."

"I do feel as though I could sleep for just days and days," Miss Stanton agreed, rising as her guests did, but swaying a little as if she were lightheaded. "But you cannot think how much better I feel for having had this conversation."

The two young ladies made their farewells, impressing their willingness to assist in any way that Miss Stanton might need, and promising to return soon. Ellen had to fairly bite the inside of her lip to keep from speaking to Arabella before they were well out of earshot of the stately manor, and the indignant energy that bubbled up within her chest kept her from so much as noticing the chilly autumn wind that had begun to whip through the trees.

"I never in a thousand years would have imagined such a thing," she burst out once they had rounded the gate and could be certain that none of the servants were within hearing distance. "I thought I was either going to faint or shriek when poor Miss Stanton mentioned that Mr. Marksham made a present of a bottle of brandy."

"I felt just the same way," Arabella said. "And my face must have shown the strain on my nerves. If she had not been so consumed by her grief, she would certainly have noticed that something was amiss. Who would have thought the *magistrate* would be a murderer?"

"You noticed that there was something odd about the way Mr. Marksham was responding to Doctor Larkin' discovery," Ellen pointed out. "You are always so perceptive about such matters."

"Noticing that a person's reactions are odd is a far cry from seeing that they are guilty of murder, I should say. I certainly cannot claim to have suspected *that*. And besides, I will point out that it was you who had the idea to come speak to Miss Stanton today, so really the credit of the discovery is entirely yours."

"It really isn't," argued Ellen. "As much as I should like to claim it. For one thing, the gentlemen were sure to come question Miss Stanton eventually, and they would have asked her about the origins of the bottle of brandy."

"And doubtless she would have been very hesitant to tell them the truth, as Mr. Marksham himself would be included in their party. Even if he were not with them, she might have been reluctant to implicate him. She said herself that she is not particularly courageous," Arabella countered.

"For another thing, it is not yet perfectly proven that Mr. Marksham's gift *was* the vessel of the poison," Ellen continued stubbornly. "It could have been some other bottle of brandy after all, for she did say that her aunt never had the chance to taste that one."

"Which is why you asked her if she was there when Lady Evans took ill, isn't it? To see if she was merely assuming that or if she knew it for a fact."

"Yes, and I imagine she was speaking out of her grief that Lady Evans missed out on the remaining years she was entitled to, but there is still some small doubt. We shall have to tell the others what we have heard, and then I suppose that between Miss Stanton and Doctor Larkin it will be a simple enough matter to determine if the poisoned brandy and Mr. Marksham's gift are the same. Until then, it would be folly to even suggest that the magistrate is guilty of such a crime, after all, he was appointed by the duke."

Arabella sighed. "Then we had better speak to the others immediately, for if they have managed to convince Mr. Marksham to investigate Lady Evans's death as a murder, he will be sure to attempt to intimidate Miss Stanton into keeping silent. Her life might very well be at risk." Arabella quickened her pace as the realization of danger struck her.

CHAPTER 20

As fate would have it, Ellen and Arabella soon happened upon a disgruntled looking party comprising Doctor Larkin, Lord Sedgewick, Mr. Millworth, and Lord Willingham coming from the direction of the magistrate's estate.

"Oh, thank providence," Ellen gasped, rather out of breath, both from rushing as quickly as possible and the overwhelming sense of urgency Arabella's words had invoked. "There isn't a moment to spare, you all must go to Tidwell House at once. We believe, we know who killed poor Lady Evans."

It was, she could admit privately, rather gratifying to see their expressions of annoyance change so rapidly to shock and interest as they drew near.

"How have you managed to make such a discovery?" demanded Lord Sedgewick, looking torn between his instinctive incredulity, and his general respect for Arabella's good judgement.

"We will explain as we walk, there is a chance that Miss Stanton may be in danger, or at least, there is if you have spoken to the magistrate just now," Arabella said urgently, giving Lord Willingham a questioning look as she accepted his arm. He, at least, seemed ready to take the two young ladies at their word and accept there was an imminent threat to address.

"We have, much good that it did us," he replied, sounding aggrieved. "I would never have believed that anyone could be so ridiculously stubborn and short-sighted. It was all but impossible to make the man see reason. For the better half of our interview, he persisted in saying that Larkin was simply mistaken in his diagnosis and Lady Evans had died a perfectly natural death. And when we finally convinced him to see that she had been deliberately killed, he became even more preposterous."

"What do you mean?" asked Ellen, noticing the look that Lord Willingham exchanged with Doctor Larkin as he concluded his speech.

"It is mere folly," Mr. Millworth said quickly. "Nothing that anyone in their right mind would ever entertain for an instant."

"The magistrate has suggested that I am responsible for the death of Lady Evans," Doctor Larkin said calmly, offering his arm to Ellen with a smile. "His idea is that either I failed to treat some naturally occurring ailment properly, resulting in her death, and I wish to avoid recrimination by claiming she was poisoned, or-"

"Never mind his other suggestion," interjected Lord Willingham wrathfully. "My temper may not prove equal to hearing it a second time."

"Or that I have deliberately poisoned Lady Evans in order to prove myself correct regarding the livestock deaths, and make him look foolish in the bargain," Doctor Larkin continued in the same even tone.

"*What?*" Ellen and Arabella spoke as one, indignation raising their voices by several unladylike octaves.

"Do not trouble yourselves," Lord Sedgewick said firmly, with the assured confidence of a powerful man possessed of the rank and position to ensure that justice would be done. "No one will credit such obvious nonsense, I assure you both."

"They certainly won't, once it is made known that Mr. Marksham himself is the murderer." Ellen snapped vehemently, causing all four of the gentlemen to stop in their tracks and stare at her. She tugged impatiently at Doctor Larkin' arm, unable to stand still and potentially keep Miss Stanton in harm's way any longer.

"We must hurry." she insisted. "Arabella and I went to call on Miss Stanton," she said with a quick sidelong glance at Arabella she decided to leave out the small detail of their real motivation in going to Tidwell House. It was hardly the time to be scolded for interfering in such a serious matter. "In the course of our conversation, she mentioned Mr. Marksham had visited recently to apologize to Lady Evans for their ongoing feud over the property boundaries, and to give her a very particular bottle of *brandy* by way of making amends."

"That *might* be a coincidence, but it hardly seems likely, given the outrageous way Mr. Marksham has behaved all along," Arabella added, matching Ellen's pace so that the gentlemen were forced to keep up with them if they wished to hear. "You can verify if it is the same bottle, can't you?"

"And you can see why we feel such urgency since it may occur to the magistrate that Miss Stanton could reveal his involvement. He would doubtless have no hesitation in causing her death as well," concluded Ellen, and she was gratified to feel that Doctor Larkin' pace all but doubled at her words.

"Miss Stanton is in grave danger, just as you say, I fear," said Mr. Millworth in a heavy tone, looking suddenly weary. "I happen to know for a fact that Mr. Marksham gave Lady Evans a bottle of cherry brandy not two days ago."

"How certain are you of that?" asked Lord Sedgewick, his heavy brows drawing together in furious concentration.

"Entirely certain, I am afraid. I had stopped by to call on Lady Evans the day before yesterday. I wanted to ask her about the shooting party that we usually take on her lands. Her late husband was passionately fond of shooting, but she never cared for the sport overmuch. That isn't important, I suppose. I asked for permission to hunt on her land, as I do every year, and she told me, as she does every year, that I was more than welcome to every fowl on the place so long as I promised not to drag her out in the cold to shoot them. And then she offered me a glass of brandy. Cherry brandy, she said, with a haughty sniff in her voice. The magistrate had brought it over earlier that day as a sort of peace offering."

"*Papa*," Ellen breathed aghast that her own father had come so close to his demise. She held on to her decorum with difficulty when all she wanted to do was throw her arms around the man and hug him. With eyes wide, she stared at him, horrified at the very thought.

"Thank providence that you declined Lady Evans' offer, and that no one else drank the brandy either," Doctor Larkin said. For once, Ellen paid no mind to Doctor Larkin's words, she was overcome with fear. Ellen felt suddenly cold all over at the realization that her beloved father had escaped the jaws of death by such a narrow margin.

"I never did have much liking for brandy," Mr. Millworth said with a reassuring smile aimed at his daughter, evidently guessing at her distress. "Doubtless I shall have even less of a taste for the stuff after this. I suppose, you have the bottle safely put away, Doctor Larkin?"

"Yes, I took it with me to run some tests, and have locked it securely in a chest as it must be evidence of some importance. There is no chance of anyone getting at it. You could identify it as the same bottle that Lady Evans indicated was a gift from Mr. Marksham?"

"Oh, I imagine so, it was rather distinctive cut glass with a sunburst design."

"Yes, that is the very one," the doctor nodded grimly. "There can be little doubt, then, I suppose. All the same, I believe it would be best to speak with Miss Stanton and the other members of the household and see if any of them can confirm the origin of that bottle."

"You are wise to avoid leaping to conclusions, especially in a situation such as this. It will be a rather complicated thing to do, accusing a magistrate of committing murder," stated Mr. Millworth, frowning.

"Hideously complicated, to say nothing of dangerous," Arabella agreed. "It is not only Miss Stanton's life that is in danger as long as Mr. Marksham remains at large, Doctor Larkin, but your own as well. He has already shown that he doesn't mind killing off those who present themselves as obstacles. Perhaps you gentlemen are not entirely aware of how servants love to talk, but I should think it entirely likely word is already beginning to spread that you took away the bottle of brandy. That alone may be enough to put your life at risk, I fear."

"And do not forget that you are already something of a thorn in the magistrate's side," said Lord Sedgewick, seeming convinced of the accuracy of the suggestion. "If Mr. Marksham is truly obsessed with killing and has moved on to taking human life as you feared might be the case, then it seems reasonable to assume that the people who annoy him are inherently at a greater risk. If you had gone interrogating Lady Evans' household about that brandy without knowledge of this discovery, Doctor

Larkin, it might have been the last thing that you did on this earth."

Ellen could not prevent her fingers from tightening their grasp on the doctor's arm convulsively at that idea. The two men she cared for most in the world—and she suddenly knew with certainty that she *did* care a great deal for Doctor Larkin—could so easily have been cut down with such a monstrous act was beyond all comprehension.

The doctor briefly placed his hand over hers, a reassuring point of contact that somehow steadied the light-headed hysteria that had been threatening to overtake her. She looked up to see that he was smiling at her even while they rushed urgently along, looking inordinately pleased, somehow.

"Well, we shall not give the fiend an opportunity to harm anyone else," declared Lord Willingham, grim determination clearly evident in his demeanor.

"Quite right," Lord Sedgewick agreed, looking at his future son-in-law with approval. "Magistrate or not, before nightfall arrives, he will not be free to continue such dastardly behavior any longer. We will stop at Tidwell House only long enough to confirm with Miss Stanton and the household staff a description of the bottle that Mr. Marksham brought. Then we shall confront Marksham and detain him. All of this poisoning business only confirms what I already knew—the man is a coward and shall give us no resistance in a face-to-face confrontation."

CHAPTER 21

The disapproving housekeeper at Tidwell House admitted the decidedly out of breath and disheveled party, looking rather resigned to the apparent fact that no one was going to respect the privacy of a household in mourning. Saying little, she showed them all into the overly warm parlor again, where Miss Stanton sat with a puzzled expression on her plain little face, and Mr. Marksham himself spoke in urgent, wheedling tones.

The magistrate rose to his feet as the group entered. "What is the meaning of this?" he blustered as he rose ponderously from his seat beside the thoroughly bewildered Miss Stanton.

"We hope to find out," Lord Sedgewick said deliberately.

Ellen supposed it was really quite dreadful of her to feel a trifle triumphant at being proven correct in insisting upon haste, particularly since her correctness meant that pitiful Mary Stanton's life was in imminent danger. But after having been so thoroughly fooled by her former fiancé, it was reassuring to see that she was not always entirely gullible. She put aside the pleasant sensation of vindication with some difficulty, but heard Arabella declare in an undertone, "I see we were right to insist that this matter was urgent."

"Happy is the gentleman who heeds the counsel of such wise ladies," Lord Willingham murmured, but his attention was really riveted upon Mr. Marksham, whose countenance had undergone a comically exaggerated series of changes upon seeing the newcomers.

He was quite unable to escape the situation, and Ellen observed sweat beading clammily upon his brow as his eyes darted back and forth in panic. Evidently deciding to attempt to brazen the thing out, he worked up a semblance of his usual condescending manner.

"Dear, dear, you all look terribly windblown and wild. Not entirely the right tone for paying a call of condolence, don't you think? Rather undignified, I should say," he declared contemptuously. "It might behoove everyone to recall that this is a somber and trying day for poor Miss Stanton, not a fox hunt."

"Indeed, you seem to have developed a great deal of concern for Miss Stanton's feelings in the last quarter of an hour, Mr. Marksham. Why, when we departed from your home not long ago you declared you were feeling unwell and needed to rest," Lord Sedgewick said, his tone ripe with sarcasm.

"Ah, well, it is an unfortunate fact that my duties as magistrate oblige me to put my own health and comfort aside whenever I am needed. That may be difficult for private persons to fully comprehend. I do not complain, of course. I am only too dedicated to those duties, and of course, I cannot in good conscience neglect anyone who has been so recently bereft," replied Mr. Marksham, actually looking a little smug as he spoke.

"I do not have the patience to listen to this drivel any longer," Lord Willingham declared, looking at the magistrate as if he were a vile worm. "Miss Stanton, you have our most sincere apologies for this intrusion, I am sure, but the matter at hand is too urgent for delicacy. What has this man been saying to you just now?"

"This is all terribly confusing," Miss Stanton stammered. "I hardly know how to answer you, sir."

"Perhaps Miss Stanton will be more comfortable speaking plainly if Mr. Marksham is not present," suggested Ellen, seeing the young woman's eyes rest upon the magistrate and her color become rather sickly. She crossed the room to sit beside Miss Stanton and Arabella did the same.

"You are right, of course, Miss Millworth. Mr. Marksham must be escorted out for a few moments at least," Doctor Larkin said at once, only to be shouted down by Mr. Marksham.

"Of all the disrespectful young upstarts." the man declared indignantly, taking several steps towards the doctor as if to intimidate him. "I am a nobleman, sir, and the representative of the law in this neighborhood. I will certainly not tolerate such insulting treatment from one such as yourself."

"That is quite enough," Mr. Millworth said firmly. "If you are really such a gentleman, and really so concerned with Miss Stanton's feelings, you will not mind stepping into the foyer for a few moments. Unless, that is, you are fearful of something that the young lady may have to tell us?"

Although he spluttered and scowled, the magistrate seemed to accept that he had been at least momentarily defeated, and with very ill grace conceded to exit the parlor in the company of Mr. Millworth and Lord Willingham.

"You must not be afraid, Miss Stanton," Arabella said soothingly once the door had closed. "I imagine the magistrate has just been attempting to intimidate you or persuade you on some matter, and it is vitally important that you disclose everything that he said."

"I—indeed, I do not mean to cause any trouble, not for anyone," Miss Stanton said, her eyes fixed upon Lord Sedgewick pleadingly. "I am just so hopelessly confused now."

"If there is any trouble, it will not be your doing," the earl assured her with confident authority. "You may rest your mind on that account, and simply relate what Mr. Marksham has said to you today."

"Well, he said a great many things, all very quickly, and none of which seemed to go together exactly. He wished to express his deepest sorrow at the passing of my aunt, and then he spoke at length about how very sorry he was to see me become so alone and friendless. He said that he had long admired me and…" the poor girl faltered, her face aflame, and Ellen took her hand in solidarity and comfort. Miss Stanton gave her a brief, grateful smile, then resumed her narrative. "It is rather indelicate for me to repeat just quite what he said then, but he suggested he would very much like to make me his wife and said that surely, I had been aware of his intentions all along. Which, I must tell you all, I had not even the slightest notion that Mr. Marksham had such a thought in his mind."

"The very idea of—" Ellen began in outrage, and then cut herself off suddenly as she realized she did not actually know if Miss Stanton objected to such a union or felt insulted by the suggestion. She would hardly be the first woman, alone and friendless, to agree to the protection of an older, wealthy gentleman, after all.

"It is not a proposal that I would ever entertain," Miss Stanton said, seeming to understand what Ellen had been about to say, and shaking her head slightly. "But Mr. Marksham did not permit me any time to make a response. He seemed to take my acceptance as a foregone conclusion and spoke at great length of the many ways that such a union would benefit me, and how he should always cherish me and shower me with everything that my heart might desire. All he asked in return, he said, was my loyalty."

"What an odd thing to say during a marriage proposal," Arabella observed curiously. She exchanged glances with her own betrothed and a slight blush colored her cheeks. "Only your loyalty? He said that specifically?"

"Yes, he repeated the word numerous times, as a matter of fact. And then without giving me an opportunity to make my own wishes known, he seemed to change the subject entirely. It was to such an unconnected topic that I began to worry if perhaps his mind might be a little disordered. The bottle of brandy that he gave Aunt Agatha, of all things."

"What did he have to say on that subject?" asked Doctor Larkin, his remarkably controlled voice giving away no hint of the importance of the question.

"I hardly understood, to be perfectly truthful, Doctor. He spoke of how valuable my discretion on the matter would be to him, how a wife's loyalty to her husband naturally dictated her silence on delicate matters, which I suppose *is* true enough, in a general sense. He said there was really no need for me to mention to anyone else the gift which he had made to Aunt Agatha a few days ago. He seemed to be attempting to insinuate *something*, but I am afraid I am hopelessly stupid about such things. I never do seem to know what people mean unless they actually come out and say something.

"Any lack of comprehension is hardly your fault in this particular case, Miss Stanton. I believe that Mr. Marksham's mind *is* somewhat disordered just now, although not perhaps in the sense that you mean," the doctor said ironically. "I believe we can shed some light on his strange behavior, but I am afraid that before doing so I must ask you to describe the bottle of brandy that the magistrate presented to your aunt."

"The brandy is really so important? Dear me, I am more confused than ever, but of course I will do whatever is needed. As I recall, it was a very pretty green cut-glass bottle with the loveliest design. He told Aunt Agatha that the brandy was a unique cherry flavor and that he had gone to a great trouble to procure it especially for her."

"I have no doubt that he did," muttered Ellen darkly, but only shook her head when Miss Stanton gave her a questioning look.

"And you personally witnessed Mr. Marksham saying this and giving the brandy to Lady Evans?" asked Doctor Larkin, his expression more serious than ever.

"Why, yes, I was sitting right beside my aunt when the magistrate came to call on her. But why ever should it matter so particularly?"

"Miss Stanton, I will tell you what I did not say yesterday when I was attending to your aunt. I did not wish to say it until I was perfectly certain. Lady Evans did not succumb to any natural ailment or sudden illness. Regrettably, I have unassailable proof that she was poisoned, and moreover, the poison was introduced into her system by way of a cut-glass bottle of cherry brandy."

The doctor spoke gently and calmly, but Ellen was hardly surprised at Miss Stanton for letting out a dreadful shriek and then collapsing into a dead faint. No one might be blamed for having such a reaction to being informed that they had just received a proposal of marriage from someone who had just murdered their aunt, after all.

CHAPTER 22

Doctor Larkin hurried to Miss Stanton, whose limp body Ellen had only just managed to keep from sliding to the floor. While he waved smelling salts beneath her nose, Lord Willingham stuck his head halfway through the parlor door, alerted by the shriek that had carried into the passageway.

"Is everything quite alright?"

"As alright as it can be, I suppose," Arabella answered, not bothering to conceal her disgusted expression. "Miss Stanton has confirmed the appearance and origin of the bottle and has explained Mr. Marksham's purpose in coming here as well. It seems that after your visit to the magistrate he was inspired to propose marriage to the poor girl, as a means of ensuring that she remained silent on those facts, I presume."

"Why, the unspeakable… scoundrel," her fiancé concluded rather lamely, substituting the more colorful epithet that had first occurred to him, but clearly finding the tamer description failed to fully convey his outrage.

"Indeed," Doctor Larkin agreed drily, joining the conversation as Miss Stanton had regained consciousness and sat up, supported by Ellen. "You may tell the others that we have sufficient evidence to detain the magistrate, Willingham, but there is no need to bring him back in here and subject Miss Stanton to his presence."

"No, wait," Miss Stanton called out just as Lord Willingham was on the point of exiting the parlor. Ellen was surprised and impressed at the strength of the girl's voice, and the warlike light in her usually timid hazel eyes. "I do not wish to cower from my aunt's murderer. Well, to be completely frank I *do* want to do just that. But I will not give into my instinctive timidity, all the same. I feel I must look into the monster's eyes as he learns that his nefarious deeds have been revealed to the light of day. My aunt would wish it so."

"You are very brave, dear, and I think you are perfectly right," Ellen said admiringly, and the rest of the party clearly shared her sentiment.

"I shall just bring him in here, then, if you are quite certain, Miss Stanton," said Lord Willingham, and Miss Stanton took a deep breath and nodded her assent to him, clenching Ellen's hand quite fiercely as if to draw additional strength from her.

The magistrate could be heard arguing volubly with his captors, but when he was marched into the parlor Ellen noticed that his color was rather mottled, his breathing irregular, and his bald head shinier than ever with a gloss of nervous perspiration. Whatever he might have been attempting to project, Mr. Marksham did not look nearly so self-assured and confident as was his ordinary habit.

"This is the most outrageous treatment. I assure you, and I all that this, none of you shall get away with such actions. Why not even an earl might expect to treat a fellow peer so shockingly without reprisal, Lord Sedgewick. I shall remind you yet again that this is a civilized country, where the rule of law surpasses any sort of ridiculous trumped-up accusations."

"Yes, yes, you've made your opinion known several times over," Lord Willingham said, evidently growing impatient with the captive. "There is certainly no need for yet another recitation."

The magistrate glowered at the young man as if he wished to engage in fisticuffs but was sufficiently aware that such an altercation would not result in his favor, and therefore changed tactics altogether.

"Mary, my dearest, whatever they have been saying to you I must implore you to not allow such vicious and baseless accusations to poison your regard for me," he began in what was plainly intended to be a lover-like tone.

"*Poison?*" gasped Miss Stanton, looking decidedly ill at Mr. Marksham's unfortunate choice of words.

"You will do Miss Stanton the courtesy of not addressing her any further, sir," Mr. Millworth declared, authority ringing through his usually mild voice. "Indeed, there is no need for you to address anyone in this room at the present moment. Rather, you would do well to listen carefully to the charges that are being brought against you."

"Charges. Why-"

"Silence, Marksham," Lord Sedgewick interrupted the indignant outburst. "Between us, the occupants of this room have uncovered overwhelming and unquestionable evidence that you have not only deliberately poisoned the livestock of your neighbors and refused to acknowledge a matter that was causing our community a great deal of distress, thereby abusing your position as magistrate, but also, and far worse, you have intentionally caused the death of the late Lady Evans."

"That is preposterous." shouted the magistrate rather weakly, his color growing a sickly shade of green as he clutched blindly at the arm of a nearby chair for support.

"Do you deny these charges?" asked Lord Sedgewick, unmoved.

"I most certainly do deny them. They are a slanderous pack of lies from start to finish, and I have no doubt that your 'evidence' as you call it is nothing more than the fabrications of this depraved individual masquerading about our village as a physician."

"I have certainly collected a bounty of evidence that the livestock have been poisoned, and that Lady Evans met her demise from the same means," Doctor Larkin agreed calmly. "But I have discovered nothing that implicates your involvement, sir. *That* evidence has come directly from yourself, from my way of thinking."

"Myself? The boy is mad, you can all hear that, can't you? Surely, he hasn't bewitched this entire company." Mr. Marksham said, with a feeble attempt at scoffing.

"It is hardly mad to notice that you waited scarcely a quarter of an hour after you were informed that we knew Lady Evans' death to be murder before returning to the scene of your crime and attempting to persuade Miss Stanton to aid you in concealing certain damning facts. If we had not interrupted that misguided interview, and if the lady had proven unwilling to cooperate, I have no doubt that she would be your next victim," Lord Willingham said, with an apologetic glance at Miss Stanton, who had let out a gasp at his words; evidently, she had not yet reached that conclusion.

"I did no such thing. The poor girl is confused, that is all. She is in a great deal of distress and grief just now, and I suppose it is possible that she misinterpreted my words. Indeed, there is nothing more likely. She is only a woman, after all."

"An odd time to propose marriage, then," Mr. Millworth commented drily. "Unless you were perhaps relying upon her confusion to work in your favor?"

"Unconscionable wretch," Lord Willingham could not seem to refrain from adding. "To attempt to manipulate and take advantage of a girl so bereft and alone in the world. I suppose you had this scheme in mind all along. By marrying Miss Stanton, you would not only be able to rest assured she would conceal the fact you gave the poisoned brandy to her aunt, but you would also gain the entirety of the property and lands that you have battled over with Lady Evans for so many years."

"That was not... I certainly never intended...why, I was only offering my support and comfort." sputtered the magistrate, his eyes fixing upon Miss Stanton in an undisguised plea.

"Mr. Marksham," Miss Stanton spoke firmly, her chin raised in defiance even as her thin white hands trembled. "You have robbed me of my beloved aunt, the last family member that I had living on this earth. You will kindly refrain from this wicked attempt at robbing me of my credibility as well. I am more than capable of interpreting your words. A child in short pants could not fail to comprehend them. You cannot possibly mean to deny the fact that only minutes ago you astonished me by declaring your love and admiration for myself, something that you have never before given any indication of whatsoever, I might add. And you moreover distinctly and unmistakably mentioned that you would appreciate my discretion when it came to the matter of the gift that you gave to my aunt. I did not understand why such a thing could possibly matter, but it is perfectly clear now. I hope you hang for what you did to my aunt, sir."

Flinging out her words defiantly, Miss Stanton ended her speech in a sob and collapsed back into her seat, weeping bitterly. Ellen met Doctor Larkin' eye as she attempted to soothe and comfort the woman, and he nodded.

"I do not think that we need subject Miss Stanton to such unwelcome company any longer, gentlemen," he said, turning to the rest of the party. "Perhaps Miss Millworth and Lady Arabella will be so good as to stay and attend to her while we make arrangements for the confinement and arrest of Mr. Marksham?"

"Of course, we will," Arabella agreed promptly before turning her attention to Miss Stanton. "We shall stay as long as you need us, dear."

CHAPTER 23

Twilight had drawn near before Ellen parted ways with Arabella and slipped wearily inside of her own home, welcoming the rush of warmth and light after such a trying day. She found her parents sitting beside a crackling fire in the library and joined them gladly.

"I am so glad you are home, my poor darling," Mrs. Millworth exclaimed immediately, rising to ring for a servant. "You must be utterly exhausted after such a day as you have had. Sit down, and I shall have a hot meal brought to you in here so you can tell us how poor Miss Stanton is faring."

"I *am* quite tired, although I count myself fortunate not to have had such a day as Mary Stanton," Ellen said, taking a seat with a sigh.

"Your father tells me that she was wonderfully brave, standing up to that hideous man the way she did. When I think of everything she has endured, and how alone she is in the world, why I halfway believe that I could order Mr. Marksham's execution myself for adding to her distress so shockingly."

"I thought she was perfectly inspirational," agreed Ellen sincerely. "You know, Arabella and I have had little opportunity to speak to her before today, certainly not at any real depth. I am afraid I must confess that I hardly registered her existence at all. Her quiet fortitude beneath her shyness is wonderful."

"I hope the poor child was able to rest," said Mr. Millworth. "Fortitude and bravery are all well and good, but there is certainly such a thing as carrying them too far unnecessarily."

"She was sleeping when we left," Ellen assured him. The pitiful creature had thoroughly worn herself out with weeping. Ellen suspected the tears had been the tumultuous storm of years of pent-up sorrow, all the more uncontrollable once they were finally allowed to appear. It had been a heartbreaking thing to witness, and Ellen had shed a few tears right along with Miss Stanton. "Arabella and I were rather afraid that she might make herself ill, crying as she did. It seemed best to let her weep as much as she needed rather than encouraging her to restrain her sorrow. Indeed, I doubt whether anyone could have stopped her from crying once she began in earnest."

"That is quite right, and sometimes there is nothing more healing than a good cry, particularly if you have friends wise enough to simply sit with you in your sorrow," asserted Mrs. Millworth approvingly.

"When she finally became calm, we were able to coax her into taking a little broth that the housekeeper brought to her chamber, but she was quite unable to eat a morsel. She fell asleep like a little child, and the housekeeper assured us she would keep watch and give her a meal as soon as she wakes."

"Mrs. Greening is a sensible and competent sort, quite devoted to Lady Evans for many years despite the demanding nature of her employer," said Mrs. Millworth. "I have no doubt that Miss Stanton is in good hands, dear."

"Oh, certainly. She said that she would send for Doctor Larkin in the morning just to be sure that Miss Stanton's grief does not endanger her health, but I have no doubt that he will arrive without the summons," Ellen said, smiling despite her weariness at the thought of the doctor.

"I believe he mentioned something along those lines when we parted," her father confirmed, his manner becoming slightly speculative. "He also mentioned that he intended to call here tomorrow, although he was rather evasive as to his precise reason for doing so."

Ellen felt her cheeks warm with a telltale blush and took a hasty sip of her tea in order to hide her face for a moment. She had no doubt that *she* knew the doctor's reason for paying a call.

"Did you uncover any more evidence at Mr. Marksham's home?" she asked, changing the subject shamelessly.

"Indeed, we did, and rather more of an abundance than I thought we would find. Marksham would have done better to destroy the evidence first thing rather than wasting his time hounding that poor girl. There were actually bills of sale for the laurel water that he purchased, filed neatly away in his study, to say nothing of the sacks of poisoned grain and vials of unused laurel water we found locked away in a chest in a little-used corner of the stables."

"At least he had the sense to keep most of the poison secured," Mrs. Millworth interjected tartly. "*I* wouldn't have been surprised to find that he had left it lying about in the open, such is my opinion of his intelligence at this point in time."

"How did you know to examine the chest?" wondered Ellen curiously.

"Ah, well as to that, when Lord Willingham was questioning the servants one of the stable hands mentioned he had been scolded for well-nigh upon an hour and had his employment threatened for asking for the key to the chest. Apparently, it had long been used to store certain articles of tack, and he had been rather bewildered to find it suddenly locked. Marksham had never taken much of an interest in the storage arrangements of his stables, nor in his stables in general, for that matter, so his sudden ferocity regarding that chest aroused the curiosity of the stable hands."

"It seems as if his downfall has been brought about by equal portions of arrogance and that lack of sense that you mentioned, Mama," she reflected. "Surely, he did not persist in claiming his innocence after such a discovery?"

"To an extent, no," her father replied with a shake of his head. "He finally confessed to poisoning the livestock at the larger estates in the area, claiming that his intention was purely motivated by profit. He had the idea, it seems, that if his neighbors suffered losses, they would naturally be more inclined to sell portions of their land to him at lower prices, and meanwhile his own livestock would be worth more. He has been in rather desperate financial straits these past few years and was ready to do almost anything to reverse his losses. I cannot comprehend how he ever struck upon such a foolish scheme as this, but he was quite adamant he would have been successful."

"I hardly think it would have actually succeeded," Mrs. Millworth commented, coming dangerously close to an unladylike snort of derision.

"Certainly not, or at least, not enough to make any real improvement in his financial situation," affirmed her husband. "That is the trouble with thinking so highly of yourself that you do not feel the need to either consider or consult anyone else. But he was quite steadfast in denying that he had anything to do with the death of livestock at the smaller holdings and with the murder of Lady Evans. I cannot imagine why he thinks it will go any easier if he only partially confesses, but then, there is no reasoning with the man. He claims that once we left his home this morning, he feared it was only a matter of time before he was wrongly suspected of murdering his neighbor and had actually intended to poison a second bottle of brandy and ingest a nonlethal amount to remove suspicion from himself."

"That might actually have been successful, for then it could have been reasoned that Mr. Marksham was the intended victim all along and the death of Lady Evans was merely incidental. It could have possibly thrown everyone off the scent of the true murderer," Ellen mused.

"From what I understand from Doctor Larkin about the volatility of the poison, such an act could also have been the death of Mr. Marksham," rejoined her father. "He seems to have a limited understanding of the properties of his poison of choice. He would have been hard pressed to ingest the precise amount needed to produce convincing symptoms without actually causing death. It is highly unlikely that he would have been able to pull the thing off without accidentally killing himself. Which, frankly, would have saved us a world of trouble, but I suppose I should not say such a thing aloud."

"Your sentiment is entirely I, even if it is a trifle uncharitable. I had something of the same thought myself," Mrs. Millworth admitted. "This is bound to be a massive scandal, and not the sort that can be contained to our own village, either. A peer and magistrate sabotaging his own neighbors for financial gain and murdering a widowed lady in cold blood. I have no doubt that within a fortnight this story will have spread to every corner of England. What a horrid sort of notoriety for our little village to garner."

"It is most uncomfortable, I agree, but there's nothing to be done about it now. Young Captain Larkin, the doctor's younger brother, you know, arrived for a visit this afternoon. The captain was most helpful in securing Mr. Marksham until such a time as a higher authority will thankfully take the matter out of our hands. Not that I think there is much danger of the magistrate attempting an escape. When I left, he still seemed utterly confident that he had done nothing so very wrong and would be able to convince Any reasonable person to see things from his perspective."

"They could send that man to the gallows, and he would no doubt be saying as much even while a noose was fitted to his neck," Mrs. Millworth said, with a pitying shake of her head. "There are some people in this world who simply do not have the capacity to acknowledge a mistake."

CHAPTER 24

When Ellen awoke the next morning, at a rather late hour, since she had been decidedly worn out from the excitement of the preceding day. She lay still for a few moments, filled with contentment as she basked in the late morning sunlight that streamed through her window. With a half-incredulous smile, she realized she was feeling almost perfectly contented and happy. It was a sensation that had once been so familiar as to be something of a default, but had been entirely absent for the past few months.

Perhaps such a feeling was no longer the default of a golden, cloudless childhood and girlhood, she reflected, but she was much more able to appreciate and even cherish her happiness at present. It was made deeper and more meaningful with the knowledge of how miserable she had been feeling, and with the knowledge that it had been hard won.

She had helped expose a remorseless murderer, and it *was* satisfying that it had turned out to be the odious and pompous Mr. Marksham, she could admit that freely to herself. She had never liked the man. She had helped to save the innocent life of his next intended victim, and it would have been such an awful tragedy for poor Miss Stanton to be cut down so carelessly before she had even had the chance to enjoy her life.

Best of all, she had a compassionate, handsome, wonderful man coming to call on her soon, and she had a definite premonition that he was going to say rapturously delightful things. Perhaps Arabella was correct, and she ought to give up her vow of disregarding the impulse of her heart. Perhaps she *would*, and then she could be free to revel in the marvelous, uplifted feelings that Doctor Roger Larkin inspired.

Her heart beat faster at the very idea, and she leapt out from her bed, filled with energy. It was shockingly late in the morning, and the doctor might call at any time. It would never do for him to arrive when she was half asleep or not looking her very best. She rang urgently for her maid to come to her assistance, her mind already fixated on which gown would be the most flattering.

"Good Heavens, it is practically indecent for someone to look so alert and happy after sitting up as late as we did last night," Andrew Larkin complained good naturedly as he leisurely entered his older brother's dining room. "I am humiliated to find that a simple country doctor apparently has greater reserves of energy and stamina than a hardened military man such as myself."

"Hardened military man you may be, but you are off duty and entitled to rest as much as you like. Doubtless you would find yourself more than equal to any task if you were ordered to it. Besides, I will have you know that we simple country doctors are apt to be summoned at any time of the day or night, with no guarantee of a break between times, so I am accustomed to being alert on a small amount of sleep," the doctor pointed out with a smile for his younger brother.

"*Were* you summoned? You look as if you had been out already."

"As a matter of fact, I was. I started my day by helping a new life come into the world, which would put anyone in a happy frame of mind, even if they faced such a dreary breakfast as the one before us. I really ought to speak to the cook. Or is it the housekeeper? I never know and what's more, I never remember long enough to find out."

"It isn't that, or at least not *only* that," Captain Larkin argued cryptically as he surveyed the unappealing repast with a philosophical shrug. He had eaten far worse meal, even if he *had* been looking forward to somewhat finer fare during his leave.

"What isn't...what?" Doctor Larkin asked in a bemused tone of voice, arching an eyebrow at his dashing younger brother. "The housekeeper, do you mean? Or my early errand? I fear I am really far too ravenous for my breakfast, such as it may be, to puzzle out such a confusing statement, Andrew."

"I only meant that I do not believe your fine air of enthusiasm and vigor can be attributed solely to a task which, if I may be so bold as to contradict my elder brother, many people would *not* find it to put them in a happy frame of mind. Speaking for myself at least, when considering nursing the sick, I would greatly prefer going into battle."

"I daresay it isn't altogether so very different from battle when it comes right down to it," the doctor, grinning as his younger brother turned a faint shade of green at the idea. "But I suppose neither one of us should care to trade places with the other and find out for certain."

"I would not trade places with you for worlds, and I don't care if it makes me a coward to admit it," Captain Larkin said, gamely swallowing a bite of stale scone. He eyed his brother speculatively. "You say, you are cheerful because you delivered a baby, and that may be so, I'm sure such things thrill you, but I think the light in your eyes has another reason."

"Do you?" Doctor Larkin said as he stirred sugar into his tea. "Have you any guesses as to what might be the root cause of my happiness, or shall I just tell you outright?"

"If I were to guess in a general sort of way as to what has made you so lighthearted, I should say you seem to behave very like a man in love, but that would be a puzzle for the last I heard you were still hopelessly mooning after the same girl you've been besotted by since you moved to this village."

"Besotted and mooning, really Andrew. Quite uncharitable and undignified terms coming from the boy who once swore to me that all color and life had gone forevermore from his world, never to return. That is an exact quote, I believe, from when a certain Miss Sullivan had danced twice with his rival and only once with him."

"I was quite right to be devastated on that occasion, for the fair and matchless Miss Sullivan married that wretched barrister not two months hence. However, that is hardly to the point, Roger." He lay the remainder of the stale scone aside.

"Well, despite your inelegant phrasing, you have managed to deduce fairly accurately. I *am* in love, as I have been since the moment I laid eyes upon Miss Millworth. However, it is no longer the hopeless longing that has plagued me for so long. In fact, I believe the lady has come to return at least a small degree of the affection and regard which I feel so ardently for her," the doctor said, his voice steady as ever but an uplifted light shining in his eyes as he spoke.

"Very sensible of her indeed. There is no worthier gentleman than yourself, brother. I hope you mean to speak with her soon, before another obstacle may present itself," said the captain enthusiastically.

"That is precisely my intention. Now that the community is no longer under any threat from that madman, I am free to pursue my own happiness. Indeed, I hope you will forgive me if I leave you to your own devices this morning? I cannot endure many more hours of patience, I fear."

"By all means, I have promised to look in on that madman of yours this morning and ensure that he is still secured at any rate. Not that I can imagine such a soft and mewling sop as Mr. Marksham doing anything so sensible as making an escape," Captain Larkin said with a derisive snort.

"Nor can I, but then I could not have imagined him capable of sabotage and murder, either," the doctor observed, rising from the breakfast that he was too impatient to eat despite his hunger. "I have found that there is precious little certainty when it comes to predict what any person will or will not do."

"Well, let us hope that you have accurately predicted Miss Millworth's behavior, at least. Godspeed to you." the captain called heartily as his brother sent him a brilliant smile and swiftly departed on his hopeful errand.

ELLEN FELT HER NERVES SINGING PLEASANTLY AS SHE ordered herself to refrain from pacing the solarium. She would *not* behave impatiently, even if she were secretly willing away each moment until Doctor Larkin might make his promised call. Perhaps if she could manage to distract herself even a few moments from the overwhelming sense of anticipation she might achieve at least a semblance of composure when the doctor actually arrived.

Shaking her head at her own foolishness and wishing that she had Arabella to keep her company while she waited, Ellen glanced idly at the volumes of poetry that were lying on a small corner table.

"Are you alright, dearest?" Mrs. Millworth asked, coming into the solarium with a workbasket on her arm.

Ellen turned at the sound of her mother's voice. For an instant she felt compelled seek her advice, to confide everything that she was thinking and feeling, sure of a wise and sympathetic response. The impulse faded almost at once, however, with the realization that she was so overwhelmed by her emotions that she would scarcely be capable of expressing them coherently. Rather than risk confusing and distressing her mother, Ellen smiled reassuringly and nodded her head, saying,

"Of course, Mama, I was just looking for something to read," as she took up one of the books at random.

"It is quite a relief to have the prospect of a quiet morning after all the horrid excitement we have had recently," Mrs. Millworth agreed complacently, taking her seat.

Ellen settled herself near the window that had the best view of the lane where Doctor Larkin would certainly be making his appearance before too much more time passed and opened the volume that she had no intention of actually reading.

The delicate printed pages parted to reveal a single sheet of handwritten paper pressed with a faded rosebud. Ellen stared uncomprehendingly at the words for a moment, recognizing her own handwriting with a dawning sense of cold horror.

"Dearest James, what a daring thrill it gives me simply to write your Christian name, even as I despair of ever finding a fitting way to address you. 'Dearest' is so pale and tame a word, it does not even begin to encompass my regard for you. You are the liege lord of my heart and soul, the only thing of any substance in my frivolous existence..."

Ellen tore her gaze away from the letter, feeling as though she had been turned to stone by the very sight of it. She could remember, barely, writing it early in her entanglement with the fraudulent villain. Frustrated with the inadequacy of her words, she had tucked the page away in a book of sonnets and forgotten to retrieve it later. The memory was mercilessly vivid, bringing with it the all-consuming sense of fascination and obsession that had possessed her for all those months that she had allowed herself to be under Sir Randall's hypnotic thrall.

Revisiting her pitifully misguided former sentiments drained away every bit of the certainty and excitement that she had been filled with only moments before. The only thing that still seemed perfectly clear was that she was a foolish, ridiculous creature who certainly had no business entertaining *any* impulse of her heart.

Just at that moment she saw Doctor Larkin turning in at their lane, his step energetic and a smile on his face that rent her heart in two.

PART IV

CHAPTER 25

What appalling bad timing, Ellen thought vaguely as she watched the doctor make his way rapidly up the lane. If only he had arrived five minutes sooner. If only she had never picked up that particular book.

But there was no sense in wishing for either of those things. Indeed, she was struck by the idea it was wicked to even think it for an instant. If Doctor Larkin had come earlier, or she had not chanced to open the volume containing her old letter, she would only have succeeded in delaying the inevitable. She would still have been the same foolish girl, feckless and unworthy of his regard. Surely it was better to put an end to his illusory affection right away rather than letting him persist in caring for someone so damaged.

Ellen's thoughts felt distant and leaden as she struggled against the return of the pervasive chill that had haunted her until recently. It seemed that scarcely any time had passed before Doctor Larkin was announced and the man himself was greeting her with a dazzlingly happy smile. The smile was not really for *her* she told herself ruthlessly. It was meant for the Ellen Millworth that Doctor Larkin imagined, a girl who was far more sensible and decorous than herself.

"Oh dear, Doctor Larkin, if you will be able to forgive me," Mrs. Millworth exclaimed before Ellen could think of anything to say aloud. "It is terribly silly of me, I have forgotten to, ah, speak with the cook, and I really must have a word with her without another moment's delay, you know. If you would excuse me for a few moments?"

"Of course, Mrs. Millworth," the doctor turned his beaming countenance to her for a brief moment, as if it were all he could do to take his eyes off of Ellen's face for even an instant.

Smiling and looking decidedly well-pleased with the situation, Mrs. Millworth bustled out of the room most unhelpfully. Of all the times to be left without a chaperone. Ellen thought but, of course, her mother had left her purposely alone for a few minutes with Doctor Larkin. Just moments ago, she would have relished the privacy. Now, she found herself helplessly, mastering the urge to call after her mother. It was no good, of course, she would have to face the thing on her own.

"Miss Millworth," Doctor Larkin began, taking a few steps towards Ellen. "I was thinking on my walk over here that there has never been a lovelier morning. However, I believe really it was my destination that colored my opinion. I could have walked through a tornado and thought it decidedly pleasant if I were so fortunate as to be walking towards you.

"It *is* very fine weather we are having, especially considering that it is really practically winter, if you think about it," Ellen forced herself to say brightly, pretending to misunderstand his compliment even as his sincerity and admiration made her heart ache.

"Yes, indeed." The doctor gave her a rather quizzical look, then seemed to be on the point of speaking again.

"And of course, now that all of this unpleasant business with the magistrate and poor Lady Evans has been settled, we may finally put it all away for good. I shall be more than happy to forget everything that has happened these past few weeks."

"Everything?" Doctor Larkin asked, smiling tenderly down at her and reaching out to take her hand in his. "I must confess that as terrible as Lady Evans's death and Mr. Marksham's treachery were, I would not give up my memories of this time for anything. That is the silver lining of such dreadful events. They so often bring us closer to the people who are most important."

"I suppose you are right," conceded Ellen, her heart breaking even as she spoke carelessly, as if she were only half attending the conversation. "Certainly, the realization that my father was in danger of being inadvertently poisoned along with Lady Evans has made me realize just how dear he is to me."

"It is a phenomenon that I have observed many times in my work. We all *know* that our loved ones are mortal and may be taken from us unexpectedly. That knowledge does not sit easily, and so most of us choose to put it aside until a life-threatening event forces us to face it."

"Your work must be quite taxing," Ellen murmured, her resolve slipping in spite of her best intentions. The thought of him striving so tirelessly to save the lives of his fellow creatures, all while bearing the weight of that knowledge, made her arms actually ache to embrace him.

"It can be. It can be exhilarating as well. But either way it has taught me that life can be fleeting and therefore, must be lived to the fullest extent. Which is why I cannot wait another instant, Miss Millworth. You surely must know what I wish to speak with you about today."

"Oh yes, I quite agree with you," she said hastily, seizing her opportunity before the hope and affection glimmering in his eyes could dissolve the last of her strength. "Life *must* be lived to the fullest, indeed. Why, when I think of the months, I have wasted in sitting around and feeling sorry for myself, I could fairly shriek with annoyance. But I will not be dormant any longer, I can assure you of that. The dressmaker ought to be here within the hour to start getting my things ready for the Season. She will doubtlessly scold me for leaving such an important task so late, but I am resigned to endure a scolding if I must."

"Forgive me, I did not realize that you had made plans to go to Town," Doctor Larkin said with a frown. Ellen glanced away, unable to bear the pain of witnessing his uplifted countenance falling.

"Are you going to scold me as well? It may just be the day for it, how dreary. But surely as my physician you must own that my health is wonderfully improved and quite able to withstand the rigors of balls and gossip. Besides, I have it on good authority that if I am ever to truly move past my previous disappointment, I must find a new object for my affections. Something that is really too Herculean a task in this little rural village, you know."

Ellen knew that her aim had been true, for the doctor released her hand immediately and his demeanor recoiled as if she had physically struck him. It was impossible to maintain her bright smile and foolish prattle when all she wanted to do was fling herself at him and weep, so she turned to the window and pretended to be looking out for any sign of the dressmaker's approach.

"Yes, I suppose that is true, Miss Millworth," Doctor Larkin said after a frozen moment's pause, his voice sounding stiff and carefully correct. "And you are quite right, your health is perfectly improved and should not be damaged by moderate amounts of traveling and revelry."

"That is just what I think," Ellen replied without turning around, for tears were already streaming silently down her cheeks. "I only hope my dressmaker will feel the same way. If she ever gets here, that is."

"You must, of course, have your Season," he said softly, his voice strangled. "I shall leave you to it, then. Good day, Miss Millworth."

Ellen could not trust her voice to answer him, so she merely nodded, remaining by the window until she heard his steps echoing behind her. The door closed and there was silence, only broken when Ellen dissolved into a passionate storm of weeping.

CHAPTER 26

"Really, Ellen, I do not understand what you can be thinking," said Arabella bluntly, several days later.

At that moment Ellen was thinking perhaps it would have been better if she had insisted on going to London the same day that she had deflected Doctor Larkin. The lie about going for the Season had slipped out of her mouth without any sort of intention or premeditation, but once she had composed herself enough to stop sobbing and think a little, it certainly made the most sense. She did not think that she could possibly bear staying home, knowing how close the doctor was, being tortured with longing for him and having absolutely no convenient distractions.

Her parents had been frankly astonished when she had announced her wishes to go to Town and have a Season. Both Mr. and Mrs. Millworth had asked her hesitantly about Doctor Larkin, but she had pretended to not know what either of them meant, and they had eventually agreed to give their daughter her way.

She wished desperately that she could confide in them, or at least in her mother, how she was truly feeling and what she had done, but she knew that she would have immediately been subjected to a tidal wave of reasons why she *was* worthy of such a great man's esteem. It would have been more than her shaky resolve could bear, which was the same reason she had forborne to tell Arabella what had transpired.

Arabella, however, seemed to have no intention in taking the same indulgent tack as Mr. and Mrs. Millworth, and had descended upon Ellen as soon as she got wind that her friend was preparing to travel, bringing Marianne with her for reinforcement. She stormed into her friend's room like a wildfire. "What are you thinking?" she demanded.

"What I am thinking?" Ellen repeated calmly, working up a faint air of puzzlement at the question. "That I am an unattached young lady and as such I ought to go to Town and take part in Society, of course. Besides, I can easily return home for your wedding, you know, and you will hardly want my company so terribly once you are a married woman."

"I am not speaking about my wedding; you goose although it is ridiculous to think that I will not want your company. Indeed, it is ridiculous to think that I will not need or want your assistance with the preparations, although that is hardly my main concern," Arabella shook her head, as if refusing to be sidetracked. "I am speaking, *obviously*, about Doctor Larkin. Why on earth would you choose to flit off to London when he is right here and madly in love with you?"

"Doctor Larkin may, or may not, considering he has never actually made any sort of declaration to me, *think* he is in love with me. He is mistaken, and I have no doubt that he will realize that very quickly."

"I wouldn't be so certain of that," Marianne objected, speaking for the first time as she saw Arabella was too nonplussed at Ellen's statement to form a reply. "I saw the doctor yesterday in the village and he looked positively haggard. I don't believe the man has slept in several days."

"It is likely that he hasn't, but that is hardly out of the ordinary," Ellen retorted, aware that her tone had more of a bite than she intended. It was exceedingly difficult to conceal anything from Arabella and Marianne when the two sisters combined forces in such a manner, for one never had a chance to collect their thoughts. "He *is* a very busy doctor, after all."

"And yet I have never seen him looking so poorly," Arabella said. "It wasn't just weariness, you know, it was a look of such utter desolation."

"As if he had lost every shred of hope," Marianne added giving credence to Arabella's statement.

Ellen's fingers slipped, and she accidentally pricked herself with the needle she had been using. The sudden pain made her gasp, but it was a convenient excuse to avoid replying, at least as she put her finger to her mouth.

"Ellen, really. You might as well tell us what has happened between the doctor and yourself. You know perfectly well that we aren't going anywhere until you do," Marianne said with conviction.

"Yes," Arabella said. "I thought you were going to seriously consider him and then the next thing I know you are determined to rush off to Town. Did he say something unkind?" asked Arabella, deftly wrapping Ellen's injured finger in her handkerchief as she spoke.

"Of course, he didn't, Doctor Larkin does not have a single particle of meanness in his entire being," Ellen said, looking away to avoid Arabella's searching gaze.

"Well, then, were you mistaken as to his intentions after all?"

"I really do not wish to discuss the matter," Ellen hedged, feeling a bit desperate.

"How unfortunate for you," Arabella murmured blandly, not releasing her hand. "I do not intend to go quietly away. Surely, you can see that."

"Anyone with eyes can see what the doctor's intentions have been for several years," observed Marianne. "So, I think we can safely eliminate that possibility."

"Did he come and pay a call here?"

"Well, yes," admitted Ellen distractedly.

"And what did he say?" Arabella continued her interrogation ruthlessly, with a smile on her lovely face.

"Nothing."

"He paid you a visit and said nothing? How very unconventional." Marianne put in.

"No, I mean, I did not permit him to say…whatever it was he had come here to say."

"That is also highly unconventional, is it not?"

"Ellen, whatever could have happened to change your mind so abruptly?" demanded Arabella, her smile disappearing. "Was it something to do with that James Tyner who deceived us all with his villainous behavior?"

"Goodness, it must have been, she is turning crimson," said Marianne.

"Yes, have it your way then." Ellen burst out, all patience and self-control quite lost. "I suppose it is because of Sir James. I happened to find a draft of a letter that I wrote this past summer and it made me realize anew that I am just a miserable, giddy fool. Poor Doctor Larkin deserves a wife with a great deal more constancy and maturity and…and *sense*." She added, but what she really wanted to say was that Doctor Larkin deserved a wife who had not been sullied by a kidnapping and ruined by the blackguard, who was once her fiancé.

The doctor could not marry her. He was too honorable in stature as well as in fact. He was a kind and good man, and she, well she was not a good woman. "His family is gentry, even if he does not have a title and I, well, I am a ruined woman, so I pretended to not know what he was talking about and prattled on about a Season because I could hardly expect to find a suitable husband here."

Arabella stared at her appalled. "How could you have been so cruel?" she whispered.

"I am not cruel," Ellen insisted. "In the long run, it is better this way."

"Is that what he said?" Marianne asked.

"Well, no. He said very little actually. He just took his leave. It was all very civil. And that is all that transpired." Ellen gave a little hiccup and looked at her friend for a long moment, while she bit her lip almost until blood came. Then, without warning, she burst into tears.

"There now, dearest, we will not badger you anymore," Arabella said soothingly, putting her arms around Ellen as she sobbed. "I am sure you thought you were doing the right thing. The noble thing, even. But it doesn't seem to have made either you or the doctor very happy."

"I have never been so miserable in all my life," admitted Ellen between sobs. "Never, not even when I realized that Sir James had deceived and used me. But do not try talking me out of my decision, even though I am selfishly longing to allow just that. Seeing that letter, my own words in black and white, and recalling just exactly how intensely passionate and uplifted I felt when I was writing it made me realize that I simply cannot trust in the constancy of my heart. The letter reminded me, not only of my own inconstancy, but of what happened. We were half way to Gretna Green."

"But you were not at Gretna Green," Arabella insisted.

"What if I had allowed Doctor Larkin to say what he came here to say, and accepted him because I simply adore him? My feelings might change completely all over again, with no warning. I cannot allow it. I cannot allow such a cruel thing to happen to such a wonderful man."

"But that is all nonsense, your feelings are intense, yes, but you are not fickle. James killed your regard for him, and it was perhaps the kindest thing he ever did. It hardly means that you are incapable of loving anyone constantly," protested Arabella fervently, but Ellen shook her head, sniffling a little, but determined.

"I won't risk it. He deserves someone so much better than I am."

"You know, you keep on saying that and I do not believe that anyone can change your mind," said Marianne in her most maddeningly rational tone. "If you are determined to believe yourself unworthy than no amount of protestation, even from those who know and love you dearly. will alter that belief."

"Really, Marianne-" Arabella shot her sister a reproving look, but Marianne ignored her.

"What you ought to consider, however, is that it seems to matter very little what anyone does or does not deserve. Perhaps Doctor Larkin *does* deserve to marry some paragon of wisdom and constancy, or perhaps he is secretly a dreadful creature and deserves a shrewish harpy, or no wife at all. It really does not matter what he deserves, because what he wants is you, Ellen. You profess to have such admiration and respect for the man, and I can see, you were irritated just now when I suggested he might be a dreadful creature. But you are placing precious little value on him or his ability to make a rational decision for himself."

"*What?*" Ellen said.

"What about *his feelings*? Is he not capable of making his own decision? It seems to me you have ignored his sensibilities entirely."

"I… I had never considered it in just that way," Ellen stammered, rather blindsided by Marianne's stark observation.

"Perhaps you ought to," Marianne said simply, rising from her seat. "After all, there are two people involved in this decision, not just you. For my part, I think you are being horribly selfish."

Ellen stood blinking at her two friends in speechless amazement.

The two Sedgewick sisters took their leave, Arabella evidently taking her cue from Marianne that Ellen ought to be left alone with her thoughts. Although she gave Ellen a sympathetic embrace before departing. Ellen was far too nonplussed to even say farewell properly, but she was not so far gone that she didn't feel a sting of annoyance. She loved Marianne, had grown up considering her an honorary younger sister, but those logical insights of hers were positively unsettling and always had been. The last thing one wanted upon hearing them was to be left alone to think.

Still, she knew all too well that Marianne's assessments were generally as accurate as they were uncomfortable. It was too dreadful to entertain the idea that she did not respect or value Doctor Larkin's judgement, particularly when she was sure she esteemed his wisdom so highly. She sat back down heavily as the realization struck her that she had done precisely the things that she resented the most when applied to herself.

She had been too overwhelmed and panicked to see the very obvious parallels, but it was clear enough now, that she had made an important decision *for* the doctor, without bothering to try and communicate her reasoning, telling herself it was for his own good and that she was acting to shield him from future distress. Hadn't she disliked such overprotection when she had been on the receiving end of it? Implying that she was not strong enough to bear any real discomfort. Supposing that she was not capable of making her own decisions? Wasn't she doing the same thing to Doctor Larkin?

And for the very reason that it *was* belittling, implying as it did that one could not or should not make their own choices.

And of course, it also implied that Doctor Larkin was too foolish to make a rational choice on his own. She had been thinking of him, without meaning to, in the same terms as herself, as if he were a silly, flighty creature in danger of being taken advantage of. Such an idea was absurdly laughable when directly acknowledged or stated, but of course she had never really contemplated it so much as *felt* it. Certainly, she believed in Doctor Larkin's intelligence and rationality.

That conclusion led Ellen to rise from her seat once more and begin pacing the room in agitation. It was positively maddening that somehow in her determination to keep from making emotional decisions and allowing her heart to lead her, she had done precisely that and made herself more miserable than ever.

It was likely that she had ruined her chances with him forever, but Ellen was filled with a sudden determination to make things right with the unfortunate man that she loved.

CHAPTER 27

Doctor Larkin sat at the desk in his disordered study, staring blankly at the notes that lay scattered haphazardly across the dusty surface. An unexpected rush of light and sound made him start, blinking blindly about in confusion until he realized his brother had entered the room unexpectedly and flung back the drapes.

"Why on earth are you sitting here in the dark, Roger?" demanded the captain sternly. It was a tone that doubtless proved highly effective when aimed at a platoon of soldiers, but it only caused his older brother to scowl in annoyance.

"I think a better question is why do you think it acceptable to burst into my study and disturb me without so much as a knock," Doctor Larkin shot back, rubbing his painfully dazzled eyes. "I did not even know you had returned to town."

"I *did* knock, several times in fact, and called out too, but you continued to sit there and stare into the distance without turning so much as a hair," retorted Captain Larkin, equally unimpressed with his brother's irritable tone. "As for disturbing you, I am afraid that I cannot claim that particular distinction, for you have already been disturbed these past few days with no assistance from me. You can't keep on like this, you know. Father told me you have had a disappointment, and you have my sympathy, but it's no good shutting yourself up in here every chance you get just because some silly girl doesn't—"

"Miss Millworth is hardly some silly girl," the doctor snapped, rising from his chair and looking fierce. "And I shall thank you to forbear casting anymore aspersions on her character. My disappointment is entirely of my own creation, for deluding myself that she might return my affections. Certainly, she cannot be held responsible for either my hopes or my disappointment, for she never led me to believe that she saw me in a romantic light."

"I shall have to take your word on that matter, not having had much chance to observe your interactions. But I am afraid that I must continue to think of her as a silly girl, due to the fact she is evidently too shortsighted to see you in such a light. You can take a swing at me, knock me down, or *try* to, at any rate, but that is my honest opinion."

"Of course, I won't knock you down, although I certainly am not sure I would succeed if I attempted such a thing," Doctor Larkin said, resuming his seat wearily and offering his brother an unconvincing smile. "But there is simply no reason to continue discussing the matter. It is done, I acknowledge my disappointment and accept that I must lay my feelings to rest as best as I can."

He spoke calmly, ignoring a disjointed portion of his mind which wanted to laugh bitterly at the inadequacy of a paltry word such as 'disappointment' to describe his agony. He was forced to acknowledge defeat, and to accept the cruel fate of being destined to love a woman who would never truly see him, but he doubted he would ever draw a breath free from pain for the remainder of his days.

"Well, then 'as best you can' is going to need significant improvement, brother, for I am forced to point out that you were mooning over your feelings only just now," pointed out Captain Larkin, not unkindly, and the doctor knew his younger brother well enough to know that he was unlikely to relent.

"Actually, I was thinking of another matter entirely," he returned. It was the truth. He had already recognized the need to fix his thoughts on anything other than Miss Millworth's rejection and had distracted himself as much as possible by contemplating a far less personal puzzle.

"Do you mean the matter of Mr. Marksham? I heard that you have been to visit him no less than three times in as many days, although for the life of me I cannot imagine why anyone would wish to do so. He really is a most decidedly unpleasant sort of creature."

"No truer word was ever spoken," agreed Doctor Larkin ruefully, recalling his most recent interview with the former magistrate. "When I spoke with him this morning he vacillated from tears, threats, bribery, and back to tears all in the space of a half hour. I was quite thoroughly mortified for him, although I daresay *he* saw nothing amiss with his conduct. Nevertheless, there is something about the whole affair that does not sit right in my mind, and I cannot seem to dismiss it. I persist in conversing with the man because I am hopeful one of his self-pitying tirades will reveal some valuable detail."

"The thing seems perfectly clear to me. Why he has even confessed, at least partially. You ought to accept your own brilliance at uncovering his dastardly plot and bask, modestly, of course, in compliments and praise." Captain Larkin said bracingly, giving his older brother a gentle shake.

"It is the partial confession that disturbs my equanimity, though. He continues to steadfastly insist that not only is he innocent in the death of Lady Evans, but that he had nothing to do with the animals killed on the smaller farms. What sense can there be in confessing to only some crimes?"

"He's no fool to refrain from admitting to the murder of a human being, not that his denial will accomplish much. As for the others, I imagine he is thinking that they might be looked on even less favorably than poisoning livestock on the larger and more prosperous estates. There is something crueler about attacking the small farms and cottages, if you ask me. One cow or a half dozen sheep can mean the difference between survival and disaster for some. It is an uglier crime, in its way."

"I think the same thing. It is vicious, almost spiteful, and does next to nothing to advance Mr. Markham's purported goal of undermining his competitors. These people were not in competition with him in any way. More than that, I would have sworn an oath that he was not the sort of person to be particularly aware of their existence. In my time here, I have never once known him to interact with any such persons, and indeed it would have gone against his continual striving to appear far more important and lofty than his real station."

"I don't doubt your assessment of his character, Roger," the captain said with a frown after thinking for a moment. "I am certain that Marksham is just the sort of person to whom the entirety of the lower classes is conveniently invisible. But the discrepancy could be explained away easily by a handful of arguments. Perhaps those particular people annoyed him in some way that was enough to draw his attention. Perhaps he wanted to see them ruined because he coveted the land they occupied. Perhaps, and I do not say this in jest, perhaps he simply grew to enjoy sneaking about in the dark and killing things, then watching the community scramble about with no suspicion of his involvement."

"You are right," agreed Doctor Larkin. "Such explanations are perfectly plausible and reasonable. I have told myself much the same thing a dozen times over, and yet there is *something* that does not add up just right and I cannot place my finger on it. I suppose I should send word to the Duke of Brambleton. He should know of these events. I only hoped to have the mystery solved."

"Even as a boy you could never bear to leave a puzzle or riddle unsolved," Captain Larkin laughed, shaking his head. "I recall the time you barely slept for an entire fortnight because the last page of the story you had been reading was torn out."

"I SHOULD IMAGINE YOU DO RECALL THAT TIME, considering that you were the one to tear out the page," his brother returned, laughing a little in spite of himself. "And burnt it without reading it, to add insult to injury. I never have been able to locate another copy of that book, and the missing ending haunts me to this day. You know, it is a particular kind of villainy to debase a book so."

"I had been furious with you, although now I cannot remember what your offence had been. Still, my revenge seemed quite proportionate and just at the time."

"I suspect the fact that you cannot recall my crime, while the punishment still lingers quite vividly, is something of an indication that your revenge was *not* proportionate. But if you are annoyed that I am unable to let go of the matter of the magistrate, perhaps you have only yourself to blame. Who knows, but that experience was extremely formative to my character."

"In that case I shall attempt to bear your dogged pursuit with better grace," conceded the captain. "But I must beg you to set it aside at least for this evening. After all, we are not speaking of inanimate objects now, but of people."

"Yes, said Doctor Larkin with a look of consternation.

"Now, get dressed," the captain said. "You need to get out of this room."

"And go where?" Doctor Larkin asked.

"Lady Etheridge's ball," returned his brother. "It will help you think."

"No," said the doctor. "Absolutely not. I have work to do, and a ball will most certainly not help me to think. I am not in a very social mood, anyway."

"You will attend the ball this evening," his brother said urging him to get dressed for the occasion. "Lady Etheridge is holding it in my honor, and the others of the fleet who have come home for leave. Besides which, Father tells me you have been informed of no less than three separate times of the upcoming festivities. Come, now, Roger, you are not going to make me go to the wretched thing alone, are you?"

"That would certainly be my preference. I am hardly in the proper frame of mind to attend a ball; indeed, I am hardly in the proper frame of mind to even pretend that I am."

"If you think to throw me off by making confusing statements like that, you are in for a disappointment," Captain Larkin observed disapprovingly. "For one thing, I am far too used to hearing nonsense to be confused easily. For another, I do not imagine that our mother will care particularly about your frame of mind when she hears you could not even be bothered to attend a ball thrown in *your* neighborhood on my behalf."

"Good Heavens, Andrew, I should hope that we are both advanced far enough in years and maturity for you to forbear threatening me with *telling Mother*," the doctor protested, feeling himself revert inescapably into childhood habits.

"Oh, come now, whoever said anything about threatening you?" his brother asked with an exaggerated air of innocence. "I merely stated that I could not imagine that Mother would be moved by your excuse. If you do not wish for me to tell her, of course, I won't. Although that *would* imply that you are ashamed to own up to the thing, but I suppose that is a matter you must take up with your own conscience."

"You are a cruel man," Doctor Larkin said without rancor.

"Besides," Andrew continued, "the Duke of Bramblewood will likely be there. You can lay this mess of the poisoned livestock at his feet."

"I have several patients who may require my care this evening," Doctor Larkin said, but it was a half-hearted attempt for he knew when he was trapped.

"And if they do need you, they will all doubtless send word first to Lady Etheridge's home, knowing that you will naturally attend this evening," nodded the captain knowingly. "Best to get ready now, I should think. We don't want to arrive late."

"*We* do not want to arrive at all," grumbled Doctor Larkin, but he stood up all the same. Rodger frowned at his brother. It was a pity that Andrew had the good sense to refrain from gloating over this victory, he thought as he stalked out of the study, for he would have relished the excuse to pummel his younger brother as if they really had reverted to childhood.

CHAPTER 28

Ellen glanced about the ballroom as she moved mechanically, following the steps of the dance from habit far more than from attention as she scanned the room for Doctor Larkin. Her partner, a positively dashing young officer, had evidently accepted the fact that she was not interested in engaging in any sort of conversation. He had philosophically stopped attempting to strike her interest with new topics and instead devoted his time to scanning the room as well, looking for more entertaining dance partners.

She certainly did not blame the man whose name she had already forgotten, but she did wish he might be a little more discrete as they whirled past Arabella and Lord Willingham and it was clear from Arabella's quizzical expression that she had noticed the pair's abstraction. Fortunately, Lord Willingham murmured something at that moment into his fiancée's ear that made her blush and smile, and Arabella's attention was removed quite completely from anything else.

Ellen felt a little pang at the sight of that brief, tender interaction. She was delighted for her friend, of course, but she would give anything at that moment to be dancing with Doctor Larkin, and perhaps hearing him whisper some lovely compliment to her. Instead, she could not even set eyes on the man, which was terribly disheartening. She had been so certain that he would be in attendance at Lady Etheridge's ball, which was in his brother's honor, after all.

Captain Larkin was there, looking both impressive and handsome in his uniform, his face and features similar enough to his brother to make Ellen's heart twist a little at the sight of him. He had given her a cool and dispassionate look of evaluation before apparently dismissing her altogether as beneath his notice, and she could scarcely blame him. If Doctor Larkin had confided in him anything of their last conversation, he must surely think her both cruel and foolish.

He was dancing with Marianne, and his expression was anything but cool and dispassionate as he gazed down at her. Marianne, Ellen could see, actually looked a little flustered by the captain's attention. That was an oddity. Marianne usually regarded gentlemen admirers with a sort of analytical objectivity that seemed to shield her from being nervous or intimidated.

When the music stopped Ellen curtseyed to her dance partner and then hurried from the floor before anyone else could ask her to dance, for she was clearly not equal to the task.

"Whatever was wrong with that officer?" asked Arabella, coming alongside her with a laugh. "You looked as if his presence was scarcely endurable."

"The only thing that I could see wrong with him was his choice in dance partners," replied Ellen ruefully. "I have absolutely no desire to dance this evening, but I could not think of a polite excuse to refuse him. He is handsome, and pleasant enough, I am sure, but I cannot seem to stop looking for Doctor Larkin. I was so positive that he would be here."

"You have changed your mind regarding the doctor, then?"

"Perhaps I have, if I can summon the courage to actually speak to him."

"I suppose we must credit Marianne with helping you to see beyond your own perspective," Arabella said with a whimsical sigh. "I declare she has only survived this long because she knows better than to tell people that she told them so. Otherwise, we would all rise up against her for being so unforgivably right so often. However, if it helps bolster your courage any, I can tell you that Marianne herself thinks that the doctor will be more than elated to find you receptive to his advances after all."

"That *does* encourage me, at least for the moment. My resolve seems to be a very fleeting thing these days. But I suppose I shall have to do my best to hold on to her opinion, because I suspect she may be a little distracted by a certain visiting captain at the moment."

"Good Heavens, you noticed that too? Would you believe that I actually heard her stammer and forget what she was saying when he spoke to her earlier? I never thought I should see the day when Marianne Sedgewick was at a loss for words."

"Captain Larkin *is* exceedingly dashing," Ellen laughed in spite of her conflicted mood. "Although not, to my eyes, any more dashing than any dozens of the young gentlemen who have failed to render Marianne speechless thus far. I suppose there is a great deal more involved than simply appearances."

"You may say that, I suppose, as you find yourself preferring the captain's much quieter and unassuming brother," teased Arabella mischievously.

"Doctor Larkin has the dearest manner," sighed Ellen, resuming her scan of the crowded ballroom. "If only he had come here tonight."

"Larkin? He is here," Lord Willingham informed her helpfully, coming up behind the two young ladies unexpectedly.

"I didn't mean Captain Larkin," Ellen said, doing her best to control a blush at having her confidences overheard, even by such a sympathetic and discreet outsider.

"I assumed you meant the doctor," agreed Lord Willingham with an understanding sort of smile that made her want to flee. Of course, Arabella would have mentioned the entire situation to him, he was her betrothed after all, but the idea her woes would be related to another would still take some getting used to.

"I have not seen him all evening," said Arabella with an apologetic grimace to Ellen.

"He hasn't been in the ballroom at all as far as I can tell. He had a long conversation in the card room with the Duke of Brambleton, and most recently, he has been engaged in a conversation with Miss Stanton in the conservatory ever since she arrived. I noticed before we began dancing, and he was still speaking with her just now when I went to speak with Lord Remington about-_"

"About a horse, I will venture to guess," Arabella interrupted with an affectionate laugh.

"I would dearly love to be able to contradict you, if only to prove myself not so dull and predictable, but you are quite correct in your assumption, Lady Arabella," returned her fiancée with a gallant bow and a tender smile.

"I should not have thought that Miss Stanton would attend a ball so soon after her aunt's death," Ellen said, struggling to repress an unreasonable flare of jealousy at the idea of Doctor Larkin speaking at such great length with the woman.

"Oh, I believe I heard Lady Etheridge mention she pressed poor Miss Stanton to come tonight, even though she could not take part in the dancing. Lady Etheridge worried about her being alone too much with her grief and no real companionship," supplied Arabella.

"She didn't look too terribly worse for the wear," Lord Willingham observed offhandedly. "As a matter of fact, I daresay she has never looked better, in spite of her mourning garb. I cannot say that I ever noticed her particularly enough to even describe her, but when I saw her speaking with Larkin earlier, I was struck by how much more alive she seems."

"Excuse me," murmured Ellen, sparing a meaningful glance at Arabella as she marched away in the direction of the conservatory. Miss Stanton could hardly be blamed for coming alive in the presence of someone so kind and wonderful as Doctor Larkin, and she supposed it was unfair to set aside her sympathy for the downtrodden creature so easily, nevertheless she would at least make her feelings known once and for all before resigning herself to seeing the two come together.

CHAPTER 29

Striding purposefully through the assembled crowd, Ellen knew she was drawing a few sidelong glances, but she could not bring herself to care. It suddenly seemed vitally and urgently important that she find the doctor as soon as possible, and she would not repress her instinct. Entering the conservatory, which was far more sparsely populated than the ballroom, she saw Doctor Larkin and Miss Stanton seated together in a rather secluded alcove. They seemed to be utterly absorbed in their conversation, and Ellen was able to draw near to them unobserved, making a conscious effort to quiet both her steps and her breathing.

Miss Stanton *did* look far more vital and compelling than ever before, Ellen noted. Her severe black mourning gown did nothing to take away from her suddenly sparkling eyes and bright color. Even her mannerisms and movements were significantly more animated and graceful, bearing little resemblance to the repressed, listless creature Ellen had known her to be. She was leaning forward a little, hanging on Doctor Larkin' every word and gazing into his eyes with undisguised admiration. Ellen did not even bother to dismiss the renewed jealousy she felt, although it was clearly not without merit.

For his part, the doctor was speaking with a certain intensity which Ellen had come to associate with his problem-solving mode, an endearing frown creasing his forehead just a little as he concentrated fiercely.

"...of course, I *do* know how fantastical such a thing sounds," he was saying, with a self-deprecating shake of his head. "I cannot seem to express my suspicions in a way that anyone can entertain, and perhaps I am merely unwilling to let the matter be resolved."

"I am certain that you would not think a thing if it were not true," Miss Stanton said, still unaware of Ellen's presence as she leaned closer still to Doctor Larkin. "There is no one whose opinion and judgement I would trust more than yours. But what is it, exactly, that you think has happened? I want to be quite certain that I understand you."

"It seems far-fetched, but I am really quite convinced that Mr. Marksham is not guilty, or at least, that he is not the only guilty party. He admits to having committed the attack on the Etheridge estates, but not the smaller farms and not the murder of your aunt."

"Forgive me for saying so, but it seems quite natural of him to say that. Furthermore, who else would it be?"

"Yes, of course. That is just what my brother said when I attempted to explain my suspicions to him," the doctor said apologetically, turning slightly to gaze into the distance as he continued to speak. "And of course, the Duke of Brambleton is loathed to believe ill of his old classmate, but there is more to it than just the word of Mr. Marksham, you know. The concentration of the toxin that was given to Lady Evans, for one thing. It has always seemed to me an indication of an unfamiliarity with the toxin, which seems out of character for someone who had been used to working with it. And for another thing, some of the tests I performed would seem to show certain very slight differences in the composition of the laurel water. The samples from the small farms and from the bottle of brandy are consistent with one another, yet the samples from the Etheridge estate is different. It is a very slight difference and very difficult to detect, and yet I find it significant that the difference aligns so perfectly with Mr. Marksham's protestation that he only poisoned Lord Etheridge's sheep in retaliation because the man shot the head off of his rooster."

"I see," murmured Miss Stanton softly.

"I beg your pardon, it is unforgivably cruel of me to mention such a distressing subject to you, Miss Stanton. I had not meant to, I assure you," Doctor Larkin said, returning his gaze to the woman's face and looking vexed with himself.

"Oh, not at all, sir. I am quite pleased to be taken into your confidence, and it is good to know that you are working so hard to find my aunt's killer, but I can be of little real help to you, I am sure."

"It is a great deal of help, I assure you, simply to speak my thoughts without fear of being seen as irrational," he smiled ruefully, and she returned the expression.

"I am sure that no one could imagine that you are mistaken, not really, after you have proven the strength of your intellect so thoroughly in exposing Mr. Marksham," she said, looking at the doctor with an almost hypnotic intensity. "No, if you say that my aunt's murderer remains at large, I am confident that everyone will believe you readily enough. I suppose your brother might naturally be more skeptical, having grown up alongside you and perhaps having less respect for your intellect than the rest of us. Have you told anyone else your suspicions?"

"I have spoken to the Duke of Brambleton, but he thinks it ridiculously far-fetched, and believes that as bad as it is, Mr. Marksham only killed Lord Etheridge's sheep. He has taken it upon himself to speak to Lord Etheridge about the matter. Apparently, there was some comradery with Mr. Marksham and the rooster. I'm not sure I understand it all, but the Duke of Brambleton was quite emphatic, and I have only just succeeded in revealing the different traces in the samples. This interested the duke above all my other conclusions. In any case, I don't have anything that is solid proof, one way or the other."

"But you do have it," said the woman with a merry and reassuring laugh. "I have no siblings of my own, but from everything I have ever observed, there is a decided tendency to disbelief on principle, and the duke is a friend of the man. One must never think ill of one's friends, no matter how convincing the evidence."

Doctor Larkin smiled at this, looking relieved.

Ellen, from her vantage point, thought she might be ill. She had been watching Miss Stanton's face carefully while the doctor had explained his suspicions, fearing that she would see some proof that the woman was in love with him. Instead, with a dawning sensation of horror, she had seen Miss Stanton's eyes, so intently fixed upon the doctor, suddenly unveiled. They revealed a rapid yet unmistakable succession of emotions; shock, fury, and then such unbridled hatred that Ellen's breath involuntarily caught in her throat. This was followed by an expression of shrewd calculation that was replaced with guileless admiration an instant before Doctor Larkin looked up at her face once more.

Ellen felt frozen in place as her mind raced, processing what she had just witnessed and heard. Like Miss Stanton, she had no hesitation in believing unequivocally that if the doctor thought Lady Evans's murderer to still be at large, then it was so. And she felt with absolute certainty that Doctor Larkin had just naively revealed his suspicions to the murderer. She knew she had not misinterpreted what she had seen pass over the other woman's face, and she knew, instinctively that it meant mortal danger for the doctor.

"Oh, Doctor Larkin." exclaimed a voice behind Ellen as a servant came hurrying across the conservatory. Ellen was unable to contain her jolt of alarm at the sound, particularly as it brought her presence to the attention of both the doctor and Miss Stanton.

The doctor flushed and then seemed to turn a little pale at the sight of her but was saved from having to think of any remark as the servant reached him and explained that one of his patients needed him rather urgently. He bowed hastily to both ladies and hurried away, murmuring a distracted apology that neither woman heeded. Their eyes were locked on one another in a fierce but silent battle of the wills, Ellen determined to give none of her realizations away, Miss Stanton equally determined to discover if her secret had been guessed.

"It is so lovely to see you, Miss Stanton," Ellen said in a remarkably casual tone, feeling that speaking first would give her the upper hand. "I hope you are well? It must be rather trying, attending a social event after having had such a shock. I could barely bring myself to venture out for months after my own misfortune, and it was really nothing compared with yours."

"Indeed, you are wonderfully understanding, Miss Millworth," murmured the other, her voice carefully expressionless but her eyes wary. "It *is* trying, just as you say, but I found that speaking with Doctor Larkin has affected quite a change on my nerves. He really is quite a remarkable gentleman."

"Oh, yes," agreed Ellen carelessly, detecting the probing challenge underlying Miss Stanton's words. "I suppose we shall rather miss having him on hand when we go to Town. I daresay there are plenty of skilled and capable physicians there as well, though."

"You are going for the Season? I somehow had the idea that you meant to stay here this winter."

"I feel so much improved that it seemed silly to miss the entire Season just because of a little trouble last summer. I have mended my ways, I hope, and learned not to respond so dramatically to things."

"An intelligent resolution, I am sure," Miss Stanton said, the suspicion fading from her manner to be replaced, deliberately, Ellen thought, by a return of her former dull and listless expression. "You will forgive me, I hope, but I *am* quite exhausted be even this small evening out. I think I had better return home, but I wish you all the best in your travels, Miss Millworth."

"It isn't the travels I shall need good fortune in, you know, but the hunt for a proper husband," laughed Ellen. "Having once established what a dreadful judge of character I am, I daresay I would do well to let someone else choose for me. Perhaps you will come to Town yourself later, and you can advise me."

"Me?" She seemed startled by the offer, but then smiled and simpered. "I would be delighted to be of any service, of course, but I know precious little of such matters," replied Miss Stanton dismissively, beginning to edge away.

Ellen smiled as they made their farewells, holding the expression until Miss Stanton was out of the room and then letting it fall with relief. It was positively disorienting to realize that the pitiful, downtrodden creature was actually nonexistent, a hollow mask the real Miss Stanton had carefully maintained for a seemingly impossible length of time. Just like Sir James, Ellen thought wonderingly. Perhaps that was why she recognized the cold calculation in the woman's eyes. Rather than feeling upset by the similarity, she was filled with determination. Perhaps it was her lot in life to be hounded by clever and malicious deceivers, and that *was* a dreadful thought. But she was not the last to realize it this time, and she would be the one to do the unmasking.

Vaguely she recalled her former sense of urgency to find Doctor Larkin and speak with him. It was nothing compared with the frantic feeling that now rose in its stead, and yet there was very little that she could actually do. He was, thankfully, safe for the evening at least. Miss Stanton could do nothing to him on such short notice and while he was attending a patient.

With some difficulty Ellen searched for the servant who had delivered the summons to Doctor Larkin and asked the bewildered man to tell her who had sent for the doctor. She was relieved to learn that the patient was a middle-aged gentleman who lived a fair distance from the village. Regardless of the severity of the man's condition, Ellen knew that the doctor would be unlikely to return home before morning.

Unfortunately, by the time she had finished speaking with the servant, Arabella and the rest of the Sedgewick party, and Lord Willingham as well, had already left the ball and Ellen could not very well chase after them. After that it seemed as if everything conspired against her. It was impossible to get a moment to speak to her parents alone even though they were perfectly amenable to her request to leave the ball early. Not only did Mrs. Millworth offer a ride home in their carriage to one of their neighbors, but on the way, it was decided that they would drop Ellen at home and then continue on to the neighbor's house to enjoy a game of cards, since the evening had been cut short. Trapped in the carriage, Ellen could not think of a reasonable objection to the plan, try as she might, and having no real evidence for her suspicions she could not very well blurt out such a wild tale before company.

Wild with frustration and impatience as she was, she had to comfort herself with the knowledge that Doctor Larkin was perfectly safe for the time being and resign herself to a sleepless night of waiting and pacing her bedchamber. When she heard her parents finally return, she considered running downstairs to confide her fears, but the hour was far too late for anything to be accomplished aside from alarming them pointlessly. The whole affair would wait until morning. Unfortunately, she could not sleep and spent most of the night in a chair with a book until the candle burned to a stub.

So great was her relief when the first signs of dawn began to finally make their appearance that her weary eyelids drooped, and she fell asleep sitting upright in the little easy chair by her bedchamber window.

CHAPTER 30

The morning was still quite young when Ellen awoke with a sickening jolt of horror. Her maid looked almost equally alarmed to find her apparently sleeping in a chair rather than the bed, and immediately began fussing over her haggard appearance. It was with great difficulty that Ellen assured the woman that she was not ill and had nothing the matter with her besides a rather stiff neck from dropping off to sleep in such an uncomfortable pose. She did her best to seem calm while also insisting on dressing with great haste, refusing so much as a sip of tea, and ordering her horse saddled immediately. But the idea of the doctor's life being endangered made the task all but impossible.

In reality not even a full thirty minutes passed from the time she woke up to the time she was thankfully urging her horse down the lane, but every second of delay seemed like an agony of torture as she recalled the way anger and hatred had blazed out at Doctor Larkin from

Miss Stanton's eyes the night before. She mentally berated herself quite roundly for wasting precious time in sleep, unable to take much comfort in the fact at scarcely eight in the morning it would be highly unlikely that Miss Stanton could have found the time to accomplish much wickedness.

"The doctor is in his study, I believe," Doctor Larkin's housekeeper said with a shrug in answer to Ellen's frantic summons. It seemed the woman had been rendered quite immune to urgent callers arriving at odd hours and demanding to see her employer immediately and did not so much as turn a hair at Ellen's rather wild and desperate appearance. "He hasn't come to take his breakfast yet, or at least not that I noticed. You can step right into the study if you wish, the last caller has taken her leave already, not five minutes ago."

"There has been somewhere here already today?" Ellen demanded, feeling her blood turn to ice at the woman's words.

"Oh indeed, and at a wretchedly early hour too. What with that and the doctor not returning until so late last night I have scarcely caught a wink of sleep, but no one seems to mind if I work myself to death, of course."

Ellen did not bother to stay and listen to any more of the housekeeper's misguided self-pity, but rushed past her and into Doctor Larkin' study. For a moment relief surged through her entire body, for when she entered the room, she saw the doctor standing beside his desk. She had not been too late then; his early caller had only been a patient; she could still warn him and then of course he would forgive her for brushing aside his attempted declaration of love- but then her relief turned once more to horror as he turned toward her.

The doctor's skin had a ghastly blueish cast to it and his face was a study of confusion and alarm. He attempted to take a step towards her but then staggered and fell to the floor, a half-empty teacup slipping from his grasp and splashing still-hot liquid in a steaming arc.

On an involuntary scream Ellen flew to his side, working frantically to return the man to consciousness. He stirred slightly, opening his eyes just long enough to gaze up at her with a faint smile of recognition, then closing them once more as he whispered her name.

"No, no, no," Ellen was dimly aware that she was chanting the words as if in a desperate prayer, and she could feel tears streaming unchecked down her face as she attempted to shake the doctor awake once more.

"Merciful Heavens." shrieked the housekeeper, who had followed her to the study at a much slower pace. The sound jolted Ellen into action. Doctor Larkin would not awake and tell her how to save his life, and his housekeeper was likely to be more hindrance than help, so Ellen had no one to rely upon but herself. Sudden determination filled her strength, she would *not* sit by helplessly, wringing her hands and crying while the man she loved slipped away.

"The doctor has been poisoned," she informed the housekeeper, raising her voice to cut through the woman's wailing. "Wake Captain Larkin at once and tell him to come here without delay. *Go.*"

She did not spare the housekeeper a second glance, putting everything out of her head as she attempted desperately to recall the antidote that Doctor Larkin had mentioned. He had come to speak with her parents the morning after Lady Evans' death, she remembered, and had been reassuring her that lingering on the path with her the day before had not contributed to her poor aunt's demise. With sudden clarity the doctor's words sprang into her mind. "*An aqueous solution of ammonia salts or hartshorn, if administered promptly, has sometimes proven to be an effective antidote to laurel water,*" he had said.

Ellen recalled thinking at the time that 'sometimes proven' had not sounded like a particularly hopeful or meritorious cure, but it seemed like divine intervention in the present moment. Surging to her feet, she began ransacking the meticulously ordered vials of medicine, the only tidy aspect of the entire study. She felt like sobbing with relief when she caught sight of a vial labeled ammonia salts but knew she could not spare the time. Without any idea of the correct amount, she unceremonious dumped the crystals into a glass of water, holding her breath against the fumes that were emitted as the solution dissolved and then she saw a second bottle behind the first. This one was marked clearly with the words *laurel water antidote.*

"Dear God." Captain Larkin exclaimed, bursting into the room in a state of dishabille that would have made Ellen blush crimson under any other circumstances, his shirt falling partly open as he had not taken the time to fasten it up all the way. "I thought the old creature had lost her mind, waking me up and shrieking about Roger being poisoned. What is going on here?"

"He *has*," Ellen said firmly, holding the bottle up to the light. The bottle was half full. Would that be enough, she wondered. "It was Miss Stanton, but there isn't any time to explain, he must have the antidote this instant if he is to have any chance of recovery."

"Do you know what you're doing?"

"No," she answered honestly, meeting his horrified gaze steadily. "Or at least, not really. But this *is* the antidote that he mentioned when Lady Evans was poisoned, and I have to assume that the same poison was given to him."

"Give it to him," Captain Larkin said, after the briefest of hesitations. "It's a sight better than doing nothing, at least."

"Hold him still, then," ordered Ellen, kneeling beside the doctor, who had begun to stiffen and convulse. The captain obeyed her and with some difficulty they managed to administer the solution. Within moments, although it seemed like hours, Doctor Larkin choked and gasped, his convulsions ceasing and a healthier color replacing the blue pallor.

"Thank providence," the captain murmured brokenly as his brother began to groan and open his eyes, his shallow breathing becoming more purposeful.

"Ellen," Doctor Larkin said hoarsely, and Ellen burst into unrestrained tears, burying her face against his shoulder without a single thought of propriety.

"Well, Roger, it seems the lady does care for you after all," Captain Larkin observed with a strained laugh, sitting back and scrubbing his hands over his face. "And she has had the presence of mind and good sense to save your life, in the bargain."

"Oh, but I might not have gotten it right. Do you need more of the antidote? I didn't know how much, I only recalled that you said ammonia salts in water, or something like that. Is there anything else? I was so terrified, I didn't dare wait, but-" Ellen knew she was babbling, on the verge of hysteria now that the doctor had regained consciousness, but she could not seem to control herself.

"You did exactly right, you are brilliant," he murmured, struggling weakly to sit up but never taking his eyes from hers. "Andrew is correct in saying you saved my life just now."

"He is correct in saying that I care for you, too," she sobbed, falling apart completely with relief. "I care for you so desperately and I thought you were dying, I thought I would never have the chance to tell you, or to apologize, and I don't see how I could have borne it."

Doctor Larkin put an arm around Ellen and pulled her close, her confession evidently giving him a momentary burst of strength.

"There now, you will have plenty of time for that sort of thing later," his brother interposed after a few discrete moments. "Are you entirely certain that you are cured, Roger? I cannot think of a time when I've been more terrified."

"I will be perfectly fine," the doctor said reassuringly, although his voice was still quite ragged. "In fact, I have never felt better in my life."

"Oh, certainly, being nearly poisoned to death is quite invigorating I suppose," retorted the captain with some asperity.

"He is quite right," Ellen said, pulling away from the doctor's embrace reluctantly and taking several steadying breaths. "What treatment would you administer to a patient in such a case?"

"Ah, open the windows to let more air in, and give them an unpleasant quantity of fresh milk mixed with chalk," Doctor Larkin answered with an expression of distaste.

The captain helped him to rest, propped upright, on a couch beside the window, flinging it open while Ellen poked about until she located a container of powdered chalk.

"I imagine I can confidently leave my brother in your care, Miss Millworth? If you are certain that Miss Stanton was the culprit then I suppose I had better go see about bringing her to justice at once. It isn't as though there is a magistrate in these parts at the moment to attend to such matters. Besides, the housekeeper fled in a panic as soon as she woke me, and I have no doubt that she has informed the entire village of your death, Roger."

"Go, by all means," the doctor said, repressing a coughing spell with some difficulty. "And send word to the duke as well. It most certainly was Miss Stanton. Although how Miss Millworth guessed, I cannot imagine. I suppose you had better apprehend her before curiosity can be satisfied, but I do suggest you take the time to finish getting dressed first."

In reply, the captain only gave a rakish wink and grin for civilian priorities, then vaulted lightly out of the open window, leaving Ellen to laugh shakily as she made her way to retrieve some milk from the kitchen.

CHAPTER 31

Ellen had steeled herself for the sight of a sadly disordered and mismanaged kitchen, and she was not altogether hopeful that she would be able to find the fresh milk that the doctor needed. But she was utterly unprepared for the sight of Miss Stanton herself standing amid the clutter of dishes, gleefully shaking something into a tin of tea leaves.

The sound of the door opening on rusted hinges made her look up, and Ellen could not contain a gasp of dismay at the look of unmasked madness that had overcome the other woman. She was so entirely transformed as to bear very little resemblance at all to even the rather more vivacious creature she had appeared at the ball on the previous evening. Her elated expression turned to shock when she caught sight of Ellen, but then she laughed almost triumphantly, the sound causing Ellen's flesh to crawl.

"Aha. I *knew* you had caught on to me last night, Miss Millworth," she exclaimed, clapping her hands like a child who has won a prize. "You did a marvelous job of pretending to be ignorant, I must congratulate you for that, as I am seldom made to second guess my opinions. Tell me, truthfully now, was it a sudden impulse to feign stupidity? Or do you have a hidden genius for prevarication, as I myself possess?"

"I must confess that I am generally quite terrible at deception," Ellen answered slowly, willing herself to remain calm even as she wondered where the rest of the servants could possibly have run off to. "Both in carrying it out and in noticing it in others. I only happened to notice the look in your eyes by chance last night, and pretending ignorance struck me as the more sensible course of action."

"How disappointing, for a moment I thought perhaps to have met a kindred soul who might actually have the capacity to understand me. A girl of your fortune and beauty could not hope to hide in drab, unassuming meekness as I have, yet spoiled and silly could have been an excellent mask in its own right. But there, you are just another common fool after all, and I remain quite peerless, in my own way."

"You are extraordinarily unique, I agree, and I could never in my wildest dreams be as special as you are," murmured Ellen, sensing instinctively that what the wretched creature craved more than anything was admiration and acknowledgement. If she could only get Miss

Stanton to waste some time in bragging, perhaps help might arrive.

"That is certainly the truth," Miss Stanton agreed with a mocking sneer. "Why, if I had half of your advantages I daresay I would be married to a prince, or an earl at the very least, by this time. Still, I shall not pretend to be disappointed with my newfound fortune and wealth. It shall serve me well enough for the time being. I may leverage it to snare an earl after all, we will see. That is, *I* will see. You, of course, will be dead."

"There really isn't any need to kill me, Miss Stanton," protested Ellen meekly. "I would never dream of exposing your secrets, indeed I wouldn't. I only came here this morning because I am in love with Doctor Larkin, you know, and I was afraid—"

"Afraid that I would kill him because he guessed Marksham was not the murderer after all? You were quite correct, and from the screams and confusion that I heard a while ago, I daresay the good doctor has already drunk his tea."

Ellen decided to keep from mentioning that Doctor Larkin had survived. If she was unable to stop Miss Stanton, there would at least be a chance that he would remain undetected on the other end of the house.

"It was dreadful," she whispered, allowing her voice to quiver. Miss Stanton did not seem to notice that it quivered with anger rather than grief, absorbed as she was in gloating.

"Ah, such a difference between us. I should say it is magnificent. To affect such a great thing while remaining unsuspected and ignored, can there be anything more powerful? But do not cry, you can join the doctor in the hereafter before a quarter of an hour has passed, for I certainly have no intention of leaving anyone alive who knows my secret. It would give you power over me, and that is a thing I shall not endure ever again. It is fortunate indeed that I came back, else I might have left you as a loose end."

"Why *did* you return?" Ellen asked, fighting back her instinctive repulsion at the calm and matter-of-fact way in which the other woman was discussing cold blooded murder.

"Oh, of course you would be too stupid to guess that," Miss Stanton shook her head in an almost pitying condescension. "As my dear aunt's sole heir, it is obviously imperative that I keep all suspicion directed away from myself. Mr. Marksham was the perfect scapegoat. He fancied himself in love with me, you know. The fool practically delivered himself into my hands on a silver platter, whining to me about how Lord Etheridge shot the head off of his pet rooster. He was incensed, but could not arrest Lord Etheridge for the act since the man paid for the chicken. Instead, Mr. Marksham was confined to covert actions which implicated him nicely, but the doctor wrecked that. I will not deny that I was quite vexed with him, as you can well imagine. He needed to die in order for my secret to be safe, yet any deaths that occurred while Marksham was locked up would cast doubt his guilt. I considered slipping in to release Mr. Marksham before coming here to kill the doctor. That would have been a tidy solution. Everyone would assume that he came to take his revenge before fleeing the country. But *you* ruined that, for I was fairly certain that you had heard Doctor Larkin confiding his suspicions to me."

"It wouldn't have worked anyhow," stated Ellen scornfully, surprised at her own boldness. "Mr. Marksham is far too useless to have succeeded in escaping even if you unlocked every door and guided him by hand."

The observation startled a quick, appreciative laugh out of Miss Stanton. "I suppose that is quite true. There was never anyone so inept as that pompous old buffoon. Still, the puzzle gave me a good bit of trouble last night, and I was entirely at a loss until I happened to remember that my aunt mentioned that years ago, she dismissed the doctor's housekeeper, who had been employed as a maid at Tidwell House. She has always been rather hopeless, I suppose. I can quite easily make it appear as though the housekeeper was inspired by Mr. Marksham actions to take revenge on my aunt, then poisoned Doctor Larkin as well when he began to discuss his suspicions so indiscreetly. On the chance that you *did* suspect my true feelings last night, I dared not wait for a better opportunity, so I called on the doctor quite early with a feigned malady, administered the poison to his tea while he was mixing up a headache powder for me, and then made him promise me to drink the tea and get some rest. He really did look quite exhausted, you know, and in a way, I have certainly helped him to finally rest, haven't I? I daresay he is thanking me from beyond the grave."

"Doubtless," Ellen said, not bothering to mask the sarcasm in her tone, which made her foe laugh merrily once more. "But that still does not explain to me why you returned. *I* do not comprehend strategy with the same gift that you have, you know."

"It is strategy; that is exactly the right term," Miss Stanton agreed, looking more pleased than ever. "Why, if I had been born a man, I would have certainly been a great general or admiral. You cannot think how pleasant it is to finally receive some recognition for my abilities, Miss Millworth. I waited in the hedge behind the kitchen garden for the housekeeper to leave. I assumed she would run away in terror at the sight of a corpse, and I was certainly correct in that assessment. You never saw anything so comic, I assure you. Then I slipped back into the kitchen to leave enough evidence that even a child would see that she was implicated. It was quite daring of me, but I have always enjoyed taking a risk now and then, and I have never been caught yet."

"Other than just now, you mean?"

"Oh. Well yes, I suppose so, but this doesn't really count since you are sadly going to be another victim of the world's most dreadful housekeeper. I suppose I *ought* to have considered that you will attempt to warn the doctor. I really did underestimate you. In hindsight it would have been better if I had made my hiding spot somewhere that would allow me to observe the main path as well as the back one. But it is no matter. I shall fix you a nice, soothing cup of tea and within only a few short minutes you be beyond all saving. Try not to make a fuss, now, it is not that bad."

Ellen could think of nothing to say in reply to this extraordinary directive, so she bided her time in silence for a few moments while Miss Stanton bustled cheerful about the untidy kitchen, filling a kettle and preparing tea. Clearly her time was running out, and help would not arrive, so Ellen decided to stop waiting for a rescue.

She did not know if Doctor Larkin needed the milk and chalk mixture urgently, but he had already been left alone far too long for someone in such a weakened state. It was almost more than she could bear to continue standing and speaking calmly to this villain who put Sir James Randall and all other scoundrels to shame. All she wanted to do was run back to the doctor and assure herself that he was not suffering from some sort of relapse all alone. Mastering the impulse, she took a steadying breath before venturing to distract Miss Stanton further.

CHAPTER 32

"Why do you have to take the time to make tea?" she asked curiously, as if she were Marianne contemplating a mildly interesting intellectual question. "I mean, if you are going to force me to drink the poison, and you need to hurry before anyone returns, why does it have to be in tea?"

"Because I am not so shortsighted as you," Miss Stanton said in a rather scolding tone. "The doctor was killed by drinking poisoned tea; therefore, you must seem to have been served the same tea along with him. Otherwise, there is ambiguity and confusion, but my purposes are best served by a clear solution and a prompt arrest."

"Of course, that is clever of you. Your mind is certainly fascinating, Miss Stanton. I suppose you have accomplished a great many other secret feats of brilliance."

"Oh, if only we had a bit more time. I could tell you some of the *truly* clever things I have done. I have always disliked you, of course, for being born into advantages that were denied to me. But now that I know what an excellent audience you are, why I quite regret not having had the chance to speak with you much sooner." Miss Stanton sighed a little as she turned to find a teacup.

"Imagine my feelings. It is rather like having to set aside a thrilling book without reading the final chapter," said Ellen ruefully. She had been looking around the cluttered kitchen as she spoke with the insane girl, trying to locate the most likely weapon. The woman clearly expected to be able to overpower her and force the tea upon her, but Ellen had no intention of making such a feat easy to accomplish. "But I suppose that Lady Evans is the first person to die by your hand, so it isn't as if I am missing *too* much."

"Hardly," exclaimed the other, rolling her eyes expressively and failing to notice that Ellen had begun to edge casually towards a heavy marble rolling pin that was resting on a table to the side of the doorway. "I suppose there is time enough to regale you at least a bit, after all who knows when I shall have another chance to speak so freely? Besides, the least I can do to repay you for being such a fine listener is to give you a cup of properly steeped tea. No, my aunt is something more like the fifth person I have removed from existence.

"There isn't time to speak of the more minor and incidental annoyances, trivial people rather like yourself and the doctor who were simply obstacles in my path. My aunt ranks as only *one* of my family members who has died at my hand, actually. They all had only themselves to blame, of course. Had any of them made reasonable, sensible decisions I would have been quite happy for them to live long lives. I told you before that my mother fell out with my aunt over her marriage to my father. Well, they were desperately poor, and did not even seem to care enough to notice it. *I* noticed, from quite a young age, and it was horrid. Oh, we had a roof over our heads and food and fuel and clothing enough, but such a dreadful quality of everything. I saw other little girls wearing much finer frocks than mine, with their own French maids to attend them, and then later beginning to prepare grand entrances into a society of great wealth that was barred from me.

"I knew I deserved pretty things every bit as much as they did, more, really. But my parents could not see that it was such a terrible thing to deprive me of opportunities. I heard them one night, talking betwixt themselves about how discontented I was becoming and how they could ill-afford for me to make my debut properly before I turned eighteen at the earliest, and my father said, 'if only I was not about, your aunt would undoubtedly take you both in and give Mary all the pretty gowns her heart desires.' You would have been amazed, Miss Millworth, to hear my mother's response, which was something along the lines of how we would care very little for such things if we did not have my father. It was my father she loved although he was poor as a church mouse," Miss Stanton said. "She could have married a lord! My mother was terribly foolish and shortsighted, you know, always led by her heartstrings. I knew at that moment that she was not capable of making wise decisions, and that I would have to be the one to take charge of matters."

"You do not mean to tell me that you actually killed your own father? As a girl of fifteen?" Ellen did not even attempt to disguise the shock and horror in her tone, but Miss Stanton was too firmly convinced of Ellen's admiration to take any notice of it.

"Certainly, I did. It was not difficult, you know, I simply bided my time a few months. After all, I did not want my mother to have that conversation with him *too* fresh in her mind. Then early one morning, I hid myself in the stairwell so I might trip him as he made his way downstairs. I had already discovered, you see, that if one is powerless, it is best to appear as inconsequential as possible. If no one takes any notice of you, you regain something of the upper hand. My father never had any idea that I orchestrated his death, and of course no one else would have dreamed of suspecting such a thing either. But then, once my initial feelings of triumph faded away, I began to see that I had miscalculated after all, for months and then years passed by without Aunt Agnes sending for us.

"Indeed, we were much worse off than ever as my father's income was greatly diminished upon his death. I did my best to make do with that wretched half-life of genteel poverty. I was patient and diligent and never complained. Until one day my mother let slip that Aunt Agatha *had* sent for us when my father died, and she had even been generous enough to offer a small sum of money to my mother each year thereafter, but my mother had stubbornly refused every bit of assistance. She told me that it was out of loyalty and love for her husband, and I saw that yet again that had superseded the loyalty and love that ought to have compelled her to provide properly for her child.

"I pretended I understood, that I was sympathetic to her quandary and not angry with her. That night I slipped the first dose of arsenic in her evening meal. I wanted to make it look as though she had grown ill and wasted away gradually from the degradations of poverty, you see. I thought it only right that she suffered at least a small while, as she had subjected me to suffering my entire life. I told you, the day you and Lady Arabella came calling with your pretended sympathies, that it was my mother's dying wish that I not be reconnected with my aunt. That was perfectly truthful, as you can see."

CHAPTER 33

"But why kill Lady Evans?" asked Ellen, although she scarcely had the stomach to listen to whatever Miss Stanton might say in response. Her fingers brushed against the smooth, cold marble of the rolling pin and she shifted her body to block the madwoman's view of her hand. "She *did* take you in, after all."

"Took me in like a stray mongrel, for the express purpose of ordering me about and berating me whenever the whim struck her," Miss Stanton retorted indignantly. "I had not been in Tidwell House a full fortnight before I knew I would never be able to endure her treatment of me, or even her presence, for however long it might take for dear Aunt Agatha to die naturally. If she had a single good word to say to me perhaps, I would have attempted to wait longer, but what sense was there in wasting my dwindling youth in subservient misery? I began painstakingly setting my plan in place to ensure I was to be the only beneficiary in her will. That was of utmost importance and took a great deal of manipulation. Then, of course, I had to wait a sufficient amount of time after the will was changed, to avoid arousing the solicitor's suspicions. When I happened to witness Mr. Marksham poisoning Lord Etheridge's sheep at just about the time I had previously determined to be safe, it was as if I had been given a sign from heaven. It was really child's play after that, prodding and suggesting everyone along to just where I wished them. The role I had to play was wearisome, but I knew that if I was patient and careful, I would earn my liberation soon enough, and I have. Come, admit it, Miss Millworth, you are happy for me in spite of the sacrifice I must make of your life, aren't you? No one has earned their reward more thoroughly than I, don't you think?"

"I cannot deny it. I can think of no one in the world more deserving," Ellen agreed mildly, her fingers wrapped firmly around the rolling pin behind her back. All the while she held onto the thought that if she could only prevail, then Miss Stanton might receive *exactly* the reward she deserved.

"I am delighted to hear it, and I assure you that I shall always think of you most fondly. You are not at all clever, and far too petted and sheltered to be strong, of course, but you really are a pleasant, understanding sort of companion. Now, I have spent more time than I can really afford, indulging you as I have, so you must drink this tea without any fuss for I simply must be going. There is still the duke to contend with after all."

Ellen's mouth opened in surprise, and closed again. The woman was indeed mad if she thought she could get away with the murder of the duke. On the other hand, she had a long line of murders in her past. The woman really had no conscience at all.

"You won't give me any trouble, will you?" Miss Stanton asked in a coaxing tone, proffering the delicate porcelain teacup to Ellen.

Ellen smiled, and was surprised to find that she did not have to force the expression. "Dear Miss Stanton, how could you possibly think it of me?"

"Stop." Doctor Larkin' voice, still ragged from the after-effects of either the poison or the cure, Ellen did not know which, sounded from the kitchen doorway. Miss Stanton flinched at his sudden appearance, which must have been quite shocking considering the fact that she had assumed that he died an hour previously. She turned involuntarily towards the doctor, scalding hot tea sloshing over the rim of the teacup and onto her hand, causing her to shriek and drop the cup with a clatter.

Ellen, observing her own actions with a sort of suspended astonishment as if she were witnessing something entirely remote and distant from herself, neither hesitated nor looked towards the doorway. Instead, she brought the heavy marble rolling pin around from behind her back with a smooth, swift motion and struck Miss Stanton decisively in the head. It was with great satisfaction that she felt the force of the blow sing along her own hand and arm, and saw Miss Stanton drop almost instantly into a heap at her feet.

"Dear God," gasped the doctor, who was clinging to the doorframe for support, his face pale and his eyes wide in shock. He had clearly dragged himself down the passageway and had been prepared to intervene despite his desperately ill condition, but the scene that he encountered was perhaps more than he had bargained for.

"She really thought I was going to knowingly drink that poison," Ellen marveled, gazing down at the crumpled form of her foe. "Do you know, I find that utterly infuriating. It is bad enough that she was so confident that she could overpower me in a struggle, but it is positively insulting that anyone would assume I would be so obedient and obliging as to offer no resistance at all to drinking poison of my own volition. I am thoroughly *done* with people treating me like such a gullible and useless fool."

"I assure you, from my perspective you are marvelously formidable," Doctor Larkin vowed fervently, eyeing the marble rolling pin which Ellen was still brandishing in midair. "And indeed, you have saved me once already this morning, and then saved yourself as well without any need of my assistance. I would say that taking one thing with another, you are a great deal closer to an avenging Fury than a damsel in distress."

"It was helpful, although, your distracting her attention at just the right moment," she said, mollified by his words. Dropping the rolling pin, which she had temporarily forgotten about, she stepped unceremoniously over Miss Stanton's prone body and reached to support the doctor. "I cannot imagine how you managed to come all this way, as sick as you are."

She reached out to support him, only to find that he did not seem to need her support. He tipped her head up to his and kissed her with sudden unbridled passion.

"Doctor," she began.

"Roger," he said as he took her more firmly in his arms. His hands were gentle as he pulled her close. His stubble scratched her cheek. "Call me Roger," he said gruffly against her lips. His exceedingly kind voice had changed into something low and passionate, and she wanted to speak to tell him that she loved him, but her answer was lost in his passion.

The kiss felt otherworldly, like a dream. It was long and deep. She felt as if she were sinking into him, like he was pulling her in. She forgot the spilled tea and broken teacup. She forgot the poisoned livestock and the unconscious woman at her feet. There was nothing in the world at that moment, but him, her doctor. Her love. The sweetness of his lips overtook her sensibilities. His taste was of heaven, of warmth and safety, of home.

When at last they broke for breath, he said, "I was hardly going to leave you to deal with a madwoman alone, even if my assistance was largely pointless."

"Not pointless," she said. "Never pointless."

"I was worried. I knew when you remained gone so long that something must have happened, and when I made my way out of the study, I heard a laugh that sounded entirely devoid of sanity and guessed near enough what must be happening."

Ellen had leaned her head against his shoulder and realized that he was shaking. Here he was barely recovered from a poisoning, and she was taxing him more.

"Here, come sit down, there is no need to exert yourself any further," Ellen urged, worried by the sheen of sweat on the doctor's brow, the greyish tinge of his skin, and the tremors that were visibly racking his body. "I forgot the milk. I was positively distracted by that thought. I did not know how urgently you needed it. Rest now and I will prepare some."

"Thank you," he said sinking gratefully into the uncomfortable kitchen chair Ellen pulled out for him. He put his hands over his stomach as if it hurt. She wanted to ease his suffering. She hurried to finish preparing the milk that might ease him.

"She really is quite mad, isn't she?" Ellen commented.

"There is no doubt in my mind on that point. It is incredible that she was able to dissemble and appear otherwise for as long as she did," agreed the doctor. "And yet, for all of her skill and cunning, she played into your hand almost like a child."

"I think a part of her *was* a child, selfish and greedy, but childish with it. And more, she quite desperately wanted to boast and preen after wearing her mask for so long. That was what I saw in her eyes last night. She thought she was unobserved, and she was angry enough to let that mask slip for an instant. I recognized it at once, for I saw just such a thing only a few months ago. When James Randall stopped pretending to be a charming and affectionate gentleman and unleashed his true nature, it was like seeing a bottomless pit suddenly open up before my feet. I will never mistake that sensation for the rest of my life." Ellen spoke calmly as she mixed the powdered chalk into a pitcher of new milk, her hands perfectly steady although by all rights she ought to be trembling.

Pouring the mixture into a glass and handing it to Doctor Larkin, she contemplated Miss Stanton with a sort of mild interest that remained entirely sincere. "I hope I haven't killed her, hitting her as hard as I did. I wouldn't want such a thing on my conscience, no matter how much she might deserve to share the fate of her many victims."

"She is still breathing, do not worry yourself on her account," he said reassuringly. Even as he spoke, Miss Stanton began to stir restlessly, but Ellen barely spared her a glance before turning her attention back to the doctor.

"Drink this. It's doctor's orders, isn't it? You are just going to have to make the best of it, sir, for I have saved your life and I believe that entitles me to look after it from here out," she murmured affectionately.

"That is the best fate that I could ever hope for," he said. He grimaced as he drank the concoction, and she gave him a fresh glass of water to wash down the tonic.

"Do you feel better?" she asked as she leaned over him with concern.

"I do," he said, as he reached up to pull her into his lap. Her elbow caught the pitcher of milk and it overturned spilling the remainder of the contents, but neither of them noticed it dripping onto the floor. They were much too engrossed in finding one another as the kiss deepened and they wrapped their arms possessively around one another.

"You are hurt. I should be looking after you," she murmured.

"You are," he said as he kissed her again.

"If you really intend to look after my brother, Miss Millworth, I hope you start by finding a much better housekeeper for him," came the amused voice of Captain Larkin from the doorway. Ellen thought she should jump from Doctor Larkin's lap this instant, but she did not. It felt entirely too much like home.

She turned to see the captain assembled alongside the two eldest Sedgewick sisters and Lord Willingham, who were all surveying them with frank interest. She ought to be mortified, she reflected, wondering why she felt a ridiculous urge to laugh.

"I believe I must agree, Ellen, the state of this kitchen is shocking to say the least," concurred Marianne, eyeing Miss Stanton, who had just begun to sit up, with such a droll expression that Ellen could no longer suppress the desire to giggle. After a moment of surprise at her reaction, the rest of the company joined her in laughter.

EPILOGUE

Several days later, having made a complete recovery from his near poisoning and suffering no lasting side effects other than a slight rasp in his voice, Doctor Larkin paid a visit to the Millworth estate. He spoke briefly but earnestly with Mr. and Mrs. Millworth before excusing himself to go in search of Ellen, who, he was informed, had gone for a walk in the bracing sunshine.

He found her easily enough, as she had abandoned her stroll in favor of sitting on a sheltered bench, gazing off into the distance with a dreamy expression on her lovely face.

"Oh.." she exclaimed, turning suddenly towards him as the gravel crunched slightly beneath his boot. The radiance that lit her face as she spoke his name filled the doctor with elated hope.

"I must beg your pardon for intruding on your thoughts, Miss Millworth. Judging by your expression they must have been happy ones indeed," he said with a bow.

"They were, but your presence brings me far greater happiness, Doctor Larkin," she said with an arch smile.

"I thought we agreed that you must call me Roger," he said.

"That is very forward," she replied, thinking of all that had transpired between them in the kitchen after his brush with death.

"But it is my most ardent wish," murmured the doctor, taking her hand in his and gazing deeply into her eyes. "For you are the most extraordinary creature I have ever known, Miss Millworth. It can be no secret that I have loved you quite desperately ever since I first laid eyes on you. I have never once been able to put that love aside, no matter how hopeless it has seemed. I thought perhaps I was idealizing you, my love making a goddess out of a mere mortal, but now I realize you are even further beyond my wildest flights of fancy could ever have conceived."

"I hope that means that you intend to forgive me for being such a fool as I was the last time you came to pay me a call," Ellen murmured, her heart flooding with warmth and hope. "That was my purpose in seeking you out at the ball the other night. I wanted to confess that I did not mean a word of what I said. I had just convinced myself that you deserved so much better than such a silly, emotional girl. Actually, I remain convinced of that, but I have been so wretchedly miserable that I am willing to trust your judgement on the matter over my own."

"Truly? I feared that you only said you cared for me because you were simply relieved that I had not died," Roger laughed, taking her hand in his and holding on tightly. "But I am fully prepared to hold you to your word, regardless, for I cannot bear to do otherwise."

"I thought you *had* died for a moment, and I thought I would die if I lost you," Ellen said, tears overtaking her once more. "Especially if I never had the chance to tell you the truth. It sounds like a foolishly dramatic thing to say, and I have said many times before that I felt I might die from my emotions. But when you opened your eyes and said my name, I was filled with such an overwhelming joy as I have never known in all my life, and I knew that it really was the plain truth this time. I cannot bear to live without you."

"You will marry me, then?"

"I most certainly *will*, sir, so it is well that you are agreeable to the notion," she laughed delightedly. "Do not forget, that I am a very formidable person now."

"You always have been," he said with a note of triumph in his voice as he swept her into his arms and kissed her with most unbridled passion.

"Roger," she whispered in his ear, and he tipped up her face and deepened the kiss.

To Ellen, his kiss was like a sweet new promise and the first rays of spring. The taste of him washed away all of the doubt of the past year. It was a fresh start. She drew a short, sudden breath through her nose. She had never been kissed quite like this. If a kiss could be said to be a kind of intimate act, something delicate and precious that required a deep understanding between two people, then this was the finest kiss in the world, and he was the finest gentleman.

He was her home and her healing. He was her love and her new beginning. He was her happily ever after.

NEXT BOOK IN THE SEDGEWICK LADIES SERIES

Marianne Sedgewick jolted guiltily at the sound of footsteps in the corridor just beyond the library. Judging by the shadows lengthening on the lawn, visible from the large window that graced her favored nook in the book-filled sanctuary, a great deal more than five minutes of time had passed since she had picked up a heavy volume for 'just a moment'. Of course, the siren's song of information had been more of a temptation than she could overcome – she had known perfectly well that it would be so, and now had no one but herself to blame if she was caught late and unprepared to entertain guests.

Unprepared might be an understatement, she realized with growing dismay. She had at least had the sense to dress for dinner before slipping into the library but had failed to realize that the prized leather-bound volume was coated rather thickly with decades' worth of accumulated dust and grime – which was now smeared liberally across the front of her once-spotless white muslin gown.

"Oh, for Heaven's sake," she murmured, still setting the book down with the gentleness and care that its advanced age merited, regardless of her ill temper. Marianne could hardly think of a worse time for such a thing to occur. Her elder sister, Arabella, had played the role of hostess for their father ever since their mother's untimely demise years ago, but Arabella, now Lady Willingham, Baroness Wickingham, was no longer available for the task. Lord Sedgewick had undoubtedly taken Arabella's skill and hard work for granted, and Marianne knew that she was very nearly as guilty of doing the same thing herself. Arabella had always indulged her preference for studying - and her distaste for conventional, stilted conversations, which had always struck Marianne as being impossibly pointless and dull.

She had assured Arabella dozens of times that she was perfectly able to take up the mantle of hostess. After all, how hard could it be? She had said. Now, she realized that statement was far from accurate. It really did not matter if she were up to the task or not, Marianne had determined, she had to play the part of hostess. It would have been the height of selfishness to do anything which might keep Arabella from marrying the unlikely, and yet undeniable love of her life. Marianne had kept her worry about hostessing to herself.

Everything had felt dismal and strange since the wedding a fortnight ago, and Marianne had been forced to acknowledge to herself that although she had understood that her sister, Arabella – now Lady Willingham really, but *that* would take a great deal longer than a mere fortnight to become accustomed to – had done a great deal of unseen work in order to keep the household running smoothly. Marianne had actually had only the barest surface knowledge of everything that was involved in such an undertaking. Very well, then, she was not considered one of the brightest young women in England for nothing, she had told both herself and her father when he had dubiously informed her that he would be having guests to dinner that evening. She would simply apply her substantial intellect to the problems at hand and everything would work out splendidly.

It *had* been, too, until she had made the critical mistake of congratulating herself on how seamlessly the arrangements for the evening had come together. She had not even consulted Arabella once. Not that consulting Arabella was an option, as she was still away on her honeymoon trip, but the point, of course, was that Marianne had not needed to do so. Everything had been ready perfectly, with time to spare, and like a fool she had decided to reward herself with a few moments' solitude in the library. It had been sheer hubris, and anyone who had studied the classics as much as Marianne knew the inevitable consequences of hubris. It was a lesson learned in innumerable classics.

"So much for all of my claims that we can learn to avoid mistakes by reading about other people committing them in stories. I am every bit as bad as Odysseus, after all. Of course, his solution for unwanted guests was a bit extreme, but one begins to see his point..." Marianne's wry soliloquy faded away as she began, unbidden, to picture the various ramifications of a civilized English host adopting the Greek hero's approach to such a problem, or conversely, how different the story might have been different, had Odysseus been the one trapped at home all of those years rather than Penelope. The thought made her giggle. Odysseus certainly would not have put up with guests abusing his servants and sleeping with the maids. No, she thought. Those guests would have come to an end on the tip of Odysseus' sword, which right now, did not sound like a bad idea at all.

The louder rumblings of voices in the corridor brought her to the present moment *again*, and she shook herself with irritation as she realized that she had wasted still more time wool gathering. Wiping frantically at the dusty smudges on her gown had only made them worse, but there was no way that she could admit defeat quite so early in her foray as a hostess. Thinking quickly, Marianne decided that the most practical course of action would be to slip out of the library undetected, change her gown as quickly as possible, and be introduced to the earl's guests a few minutes late, but decently attired, at least. She was not one to primp and dawdle. She could dress quickly.

Of course, that brought up the problem of *how* to slip away undetected, since the guests were evidently at the very threshold of the library. Indeed, the heavy iron handle of the doors began turning before she could so much as take a step. To her utter horror, the cheerfully handsome face of the dashing Captain Andrew Larkin appeared in the doorway, glancing carelessly back at his companions, and continuing some conversation with them even as he partially opened the door.

Mortification rolled over Marianne in waves – of all the gentlemen in the world, why did it have to be *him* to catch her in such a state?

Order your copy at Amazon: Lady Marianne and the Captain

Want Even More Regency Romance…

Follow Isabella Thorne on BookBub
https://www.bookbub.com/profile/isabella-thorne

Sign up for my VIP Reader List!
at
https://isabellathorne.com/

Receive weekly updates from Isabella and an Exclusive Free Story

Like Isabella Thorne on Facebook
https://www.facebook.com/isabellathorneauthor/

SNEAK PEEK

~.~

Continue reading for a SNEAK PEEK of:

The Duke's Winter Promise - A Christmas Regency Romance
(Ladies of the North)

THE DUKE'S WINTER
PROMISE

Miss Emily Ingram woke to a drizzle on a fine December morning in the English countryside. The pattern of raindrops on the rooftop brought a comfort and solace to her soul that could only be attributed to the depths of her British roots.

The cold rain matched Emily's mood. She was here. In the country, away from London and all of her problems, she told herself. She should be happy. Instead, she felt bothered.

She supposed it was hard to feel beautiful in weather such as this. She paused with brush in hand. The rain had made the fine strands of her hair as limp as a dishcloth.

Emily sighed. She would have to call her maid to do something with the locks. It hung in strings. Surely a grown woman should be able to brush her own hair, she thought as she rang the bell. She was on the cusp of womanhood. Perhaps, that was what bothered her most.

Emily made her way over to the armoire to find her gowns hung in a neat row by the attentive servants. The room smelled of lemon oil and polish, fresh and well maintained. The once-vocal chamber door now glided on smooth hinges, the product of proper oil application and keen observation.

It pleased Emily to know that her aunt and uncle were still capable of running Sandstowe Hill and that the manor had not fallen into disrepair as they aged. Of course, she thought, Cousin William took care of things, since he would one day inherit. Cousin William was a year younger than Emily and had already taken up the yoke of adulthood.

Mother thought she was an adult, Emily reminded herself. Father was determined to marry her off by the spring. Yet, Emily did not feel equal to the task. Had she not already had a London season? Had she not attended the finest of finishing schools? In spite of her mother's thoughtful advice and her instructors' careful teaching, Emily still felt unfinished.

She had never thought of herself as beautiful. She was interesting and unique, but not beautiful. She thought of all the girls who were dull, even in their youth, and thought things could be worse. She was distinctive. Emily was never dull.

Womanhood must come easily to them, she imagined. These imaginary dullards would embrace adulthood and all the rules set by previous generations of gloomy adults. It was the path all young girls must take as they became women. She must do the same. She had very nearly set her mind to it.

"I *have* set my mind to it," she hissed. "I must."

Carrie peeked into the room. "What must you do, miss?" The lady's maid asked.

"I must make some semblance of order of this hair," Emily replied touching the strands although the true problem was not her hair. It was the whole issue of finding a husband and becoming a wife. The entire notion was so very permanent.

"Oh posh," said Carrie with a wave of her hand. "That is my job. Yours is to make pretty conversation, and catch a fine husband."

Carrie's words made Emily's stomach turn.

Carrie took up the brush. "Sit now, miss. I shall make short work of it."

"Thank you, Carrie. Will you miss London?" Emily asked her.

"Oh, no, miss. My sister is here in Northwickshire, my mum as well. I haven't seen my little brothers in an age."

"Oh." Emily had forgotten that Carrie had family in the Northwickshire district. The girl fit in so well in London, and rivaled the very best of lady's maids with her talents. Emily sometimes forgot Carrie's humble beginnings. She had kept the girl away from her family for too long.

She had been gone for far too long as well, but her parents were adamant that she marry this season.

Emily's father, the Viscount of Kentleworth, was an active member of the court and a resident of Grosvenor Square. He rarely abandoned his post for fear that some catastrophe or other might strike in his absence. Mother stayed by his side. As a result, the Ingram offspring, Emily and her brother Edmund, had often taken their holidays with their maternal Aunt Agnes and her husband, Uncle Cecil, the Earl of Stratton.

Uncle Cecil's northern home at Sandstowe Hill provided a reprieve from the expectations of high society and a haven for the genteel youth of the area. Uncle Cecil and Aunt Agnes had no children of their own and seemed to welcome everyone else's, but Emily reminded herself, she was no longer a child.

She had other obligations although Aunt Agnes would not push her to it like her mother would. She would allow Emily her holiday, but there were visits to make and people to see.

"Are you going to go skating?" Carrie asked. "I've heard that the pond is nearly frozen over, although I cannot testify to the thickness of the ice."

"Perhaps later in the week," Emily said. "I want to be sure it is thick enough to hold."

"Ah, let some of those towering gents go first," Carrie teased. "If it should hold them, it should hold you. Or perhaps if you were to lose your balance it is the gentleman who would do the holding." Carrie giggled.

Emily smiled, but that was not why she wished to go skating, at least not entirely.

During the years of their childhood, Emily and Edmund had spent their days gallivanting across the sodden fields with Cousin William and the children of all the neighboring country manors within riding distance.

Edmund could most often be found in the company of Alexander Burgess, the son of the Duke of Bramblewood, from the neighboring estate to the North. Emily was friends with Anne and Eliza Albright, the daughters of the Aldbrick Viscountcy to the Southwest, as well as Henrietta Milford, daughter of Baron Shudley.

Both Emily and her brother had fostered many life-long friendships, although some of those friendships had been maintained only through correspondence over the last years. Emily dearly missed her Northwickshire friends.

While Emily had been sent to finishing school, Edmund, with all the freedoms that his gender allowed, had continued to make the journey to Northwickshire on an annual basis, usually with Alexander by his side.

Edmund used any and every excuse to slip the confines of the cobbled streets of London, and mostly the harsh authoritarian nature of their father. Emily was lucky that Father considered his daughter in his wife's purview.

Lord Kentleworth felt his job was molding his son into a shadow of himself. Emily could not fault him. He was a good man, but Edmund was not his father. Edmund's best and most successful excursion was the week long opportunity to take provisions from London to his northern relations.

Emily envied him. She knew her mother would never have allowed her such freedoms. There was a bout of influenza in the town of Northwick the year past. Rumors had filtered south to London that several people had died of the illness.

Emily worried greatly for her aunt and uncle who were getting on in years. She had wanted to come and help, but Mother's crippling fear of contagions had put a stop to all thought of visits. Emily's maternal grandmother had passed of such a sudden fever years ago, and Lady Kentleworth was terrified of the infection.

She ordered her children home to London although Edmund had simply stayed on with the other gentlemen outside of the town proper in spite of his mother's displeasure. Gentlemen, as it were, were often allowed, to do as they please, or so her father would say to silence his wife, and then he would chide his son for failing to attend when he spoke of politics.

It was no wonder Edmund escaped to Northwickshire at every opportunity. Especially now, that the danger from the influenza was past.

"Who has come to winter in Northwick?" Emily asked Carrie.

"Well, I'm sure I don't know," Carrie said.

"Come now. I am sure that Mrs. Tanner was bending your ear with the news," Emily said. She knew the cook was a fount of gossip.

Carrie shrugged. "Your brother, of course, and the young Mr. Singer. And his sisters, the poor dears, losing their mum. Mrs. Tanner was speaking of her this morning. Christmas will be hard for them at their age."

Emily thought losing one's mother at any age was difficult.

She had heard of the bout of influenza that claimed Cousin William's mother, Kate. His father Mr. Singer had died years ago so now the sole responsibility of his sisters rested with him.

"I'm sure it will be good to see Miss Albright," Carrie said.

That made Emily smile. She was forever thankful that one friend from her childhood exploits was sent off to school as well, her dear friend Anne Albright. Through Anne, Emily tried to keep abreast of the news in Northwickshire, but after school was completed, both Anne and Emily had gone on with their lives.

Emily had traveled to London for the Season and Anne returned to the country. In spite of their attempts to stay in touch, they both grew apart until Emily worried there was little left that might be shared.

Besides, Anne was a terrible letter writer. Despite regular correspondence, Emily gleaned more from the pages written by Anne's mother, the Lady Aldbrick who was more like to speak of her own friends and family than the goings on of the younger generation.

"I shall be glad to see her, and the others. Have you word of Alexander?"

"I am sure I do not know of the young lord."

Emily nodded. Of course Carrie would have no way of knowing. Emily would just have to wait and see, but it had been so long since she had seen the duke's son, she thought she might not recognize him at all.

No, she told herself. Alexander, she would recognize no matter how he changed in the journey from childhood to adulthood, but would he recognize her? Would he even care to see her? The thought filled her with nervous anticipation.

She remembered the last winter before she and Anne had gone to finishing school. Everything changed after that. They were children no more, but that last winter they had gone skating and sledding nearly every day, staying out until darkness called them home; Edmund, Anne, Alexander and herself.

Their skin became raw from the wind and the cold, and Aunt Agnes fretted. They had not cared. Edmund would wake Emily first thing in the morning with a pounding upon her door.

They would bundle up, never enough to ease Aunt Agnes' anxious mind, before they would race out the doorway invariably forgetting something that Aunt Agnes had reminded them of at least a dozen times. As long as they had their skates to tie on over their boots, that was all that mattered.

Emily remembered a day when it was particularly cold. Edmund and Anne were racing back and forth, trying to put each other off balance, but they had not a care, not a worry that they could be hurt. The world was theirs.

Emily had wanted to sit for a moment. She simply collapsed in a snow bank and stared up at the branches of the pines above her. It was a beautiful day, full of sunshine although still cold. Emily remembered watching the friendly quarrels, content in the juxtaposition of the bright sunshine and the icy cushion beneath her. Eventually, Alexander flopped down beside her, winded from his own skating.

Alexander complained that Edmund was no fun when Anne was present. "Anne goads him into these harebrained ideas," he said cheekily. "Silly girls."

"Silly, are we? And none of the schemes are ever Ed's fault or yours? You tease." Emily replied with fire, knowing full well that the boys gave as good as they got.

"Not at all," Alexander laughed. "We are gentlemen, and Mother says a gentleman must never tease a lady."

"And we are ladies," Emily countered, thinking with excitement that the next autumn she would be in finishing school. She would indeed be a lady, but not yet.

Somehow a handful of snow was tossed and there was a grand snowball fight, girls against the boys. They had rushed off in pairs: Anne and Emily. The girls took the high ground for the boys could throw further. It was the only gentlemanly way to proceed, Anne had insisted.

"And you should not give the ladies the side with the sun in their eyes," she added.

Edmund and Alexander graciously agreed and soon the battle of the century began. The girls were making a go of it, especially when Henrietta joined their side; until William joined the boys. William was taller and his longer reach added distance to the boy's snowballs. The girls were pummeled, but when they admitted defeat, the boys helped them brush snow from their cloaks.

"You alright, Em?" Alexander had asked, even then watchful and careful of others, so unlike his brutish father. He had taken off his hat and brushed back his sweat damp curls and jammed the cap back on his unruly locks.

"Are you cold?" he asked.

"Just my hands." Emily tucked her gloved hands into the sleeves of her coat and smiled up at him. Alexander held her hands in his and afterwards he had always remembered to bring an extra pair of mittens.

Emily remembered it as the last innocent touch she and the duke's son had shared. It was an end of childhood. The following winter Emily was home on holiday from school, but the Christmas season was a solemn affair spent in London with her parents.

Emily missed those carefree days in Northwickshire. Days when waking to the fullness of the day brought a fresh surge of excitement for a new adventure, rather than dread at what new suitor Mother had found, along with the reminder that Emily was an adult now, and ought to get on with things.

Emily looked at her visage in the glass. She was dressed in a warm woolen gown of forest green. The color looked exquisite on her and it was properly festive for the season.

A matching ribbon gathered her long tresses up into a neat knot at the nape of her neck and completed the ensemble. Her chestnut strands had darkened over the years, leaving bronze highlights that danced in the light and matched the flecks in her amber eyes.

Gone were the too-long limbs and childish freckles. No longer did her feet get caught up in the hems of her dresses nor did the careful pinning of her locks take a wayward tumble down her back after a mid-day slide on the sledding hill with the duke's son.

Emily looked quite presentable, a proper country lady. Would Alexander have changed as well? The thought excited her. Emily had not seen him in years. She could only picture the shy somewhat awkward boy she once knew.

Emily thanked Carrie for her assistance and the maid bobbed a curtsey. "Is Aunt Agnes awake?" Emily asked.

"I believe so, miss." Carrie replied. "Lainie took tea up to her only a little while ago." Lainie was Aunt Agnes' ancient maid. Emily marveled that the woman could still climb the stairs.

Carrie continued. "But I'm sure Lady Stratton will be in the breakfast room shortly. Your uncle awaits her."

"Very good. You may take the day off and enjoy the countryside or visit with your relatives." Carrie must not have seen them for as long as Emily had been away.

"Thank you, miss." Carrie broke into an excited smile.

Emily knew that there would be little for the maid to do here in the country where no one stood upon ceremony. Carrie shut the door softly behind her and Emily went back to her musings. It felt strange that there was no hurry to be anywhere, no breakfasts or balls called her to rush.

No matter that most of her life had most recently been spent in London, she felt at peace here in the country in her childhood bedroom. The blue curtains that draped her bed were the same that she had slept beneath during her most recent visit several years prior.

Perhaps it was this room that made her long for the days of her childhood. The summers or winter holidays spent living life to the fullest. She was older now and ought to be thinking of marriage, rather than childhood games. Not that her mother would ever allow her to forget.

Emily fully expected daily letters from her mother asking whether or not she had made a decision between Robert Hawthorne, Reginald Beatram, or some other fine London gent. Emily could put aside the letters, but she remembered the conversations with distress.

"Robert Hawthorne will be an earl one day," her mother said firmly.

Emily nodded, but silently she thought, only if his ogre of a grandfather ever shuffles off this mortal coil.

She was quite sure that Robert Hawthorne's father, Lord Hanway, thought he would be an earl one day too, but Lord Hanway was over fifty with no sign of Lord Thornwood giving the reins to him. Instead, the old man kept the entire family under his thumb, and Emily feared that if she married him, she would be under Robert's thumb.

"What of Lord Barton? Reginald is kind, if not strictly handsome, and his sister is a joy."

Her mother was right. Emily did not find Reginald handsome. Oh he was personable enough, but with her chestnut hair and his, just this side of ginger, they would raise a brood of carrot topped, freckled faced children who would be mercilessly teased for their ginger hair just as she had been.

Emily could not willingly be party to torture. Besides, she could not quite wrap her mind around the thought; children with Lord Barton. He was nice, but the thought of kissing him, left her cool.

She liked both gentlemen well enough, and she adored their sisters, but she was not in love with either of the men.

Her mother continued naming others and their attributes, including Cousin William and Emily had finally put her foot down, flatly refusing. Cousin William was Uncle Cecil's nephew.

Mother pointed out that they were not related by blood, and since it was most unlikely for her aunt and uncle to produce a son at this late date, when Uncle Cecil passed, William would inherit Sandstowe Hill and be made the earl. Still, William felt like a brother to her. Emily could no sooner marry Cousin William than she could Edmund.

She pushed the thought away with a smile.

Lady Kentleworth had continued with her list of names of eligible gentlemen. Emily had gone to wool gathering, but she knew she must eventually come back to reality.

She could not deny Cousin William would be a catch, as would her brother Edmund, but the thought seemed as strange as considering young Alexander as a suitor. Perhaps when they were all older and responsible enough to inherit it would make a difference.

William would have the Stratton Earldom, Edmund would have the Kentleworth Viscountcy and Alexander would be made the Duke of Bramblewood. Emily smiled at the thought. She could not quite imagine Alexander with his shy smile as the formidable duke. Still, William had settled into his responsibilities. Alexander must one day grow up as well.

"Emily," she said to herself. "You are a woman grown. It is time to settle into your own responsibilities. Mother is right." She sighed. "Isn't she always?" Emily traced her fingers over the ribboned edge of the curtains and flicked them away. If only she could push her willful thoughts away as easily as the curtains.

She promised herself, one last Christmas enjoying the country. One last holiday before she would be packaged and parceled away to a husband.

Emily would enjoy her visit to Northwickshire in spite of the current inclement weather. Until such a time as she returned to London, she would collect as many memories as time would permit: memories to last a lifetime.

Afterwards she would return to London. She would do as she ought and take responsibility upon her shoulders. She would make her choice of a husband and submit to society's expectation.

It would not be such a hardship, she told herself. She liked order in her life. It was the way of things. Like her mother, and all ladies before her, Emily must put childish things aside and henceforth be a proper lady. But not yet. She was on holiday.

Printed in Great Britain
by Amazon